To Karen,

Great to meet you.

MEMORIAL TALES

Craig O'Connor

MEMORIAL TALES

Copyright 2012 by Craig O'Connor

Printed in the United States Of America

Other books by Craig O'Connor

Happy Holidays

The Whitechapel Five

The Monster Of Modern Times

www.craigoconnor.info

I would like to acknowledge the writers who have shaped my strange personality:

Douglas Adams
Ambrose Bierce
Robert Bloch
Ray Bradbury
Lewis Carroll
Dame Agatha Christie
Russell T. Davies
Sir Arthur Conan Doyle
Harlan Ellison
Jack Finney
Neil Gaiman
Theodor Geisel
Terry Gilliam
Jacob & Wilhelm Grimm
John Hayward
Joseph Heller
Shirley Jackson
Franz Kafka
Stephen King
Sheridan LeFanu
C.S. Lewis
H.P. Lovecraft
Richard Matheson
Stephen Moffat
Christopher Moore
Edgar Allan Poe
J.K. Rowling
Rod Serling
Robert Louis Stevenson
Orson Welles

Hearts may stop, but the tales continue.

Into The Deep... The Color Is Black...

Prologue: The Café

The Memorial Café stood across the street from the entrance to Juniper Hill cemetery. It had been there so long that people sometimes wondered if the café was named because of its proximity to Juniper Hill or if the city had put the cemetery there to enhance the café. As far as the locals knew, it was one of few businesses that had been in existence for all of their lives and even those who never crossed its threshold subconsciously found the presence of the café to be of great comfort. The fact that it had kept its doors open for all these years gave the old building a certain resilient pride: stores at the mall might come and go, but certain things remained even in the craziest of economies. Of course, the café's persistent good fortune had always depended on visitors to Juniper Hill deciding that a nice, quiet place to sit and reflect on the nature of life and loss was just the thing they needed (that and a piping-hot coffee). The dead never moved out of Juniper Hill, their friends and family never failed to visit them, and the café never went out of business. You didn't have to be bereaved to go to the Memorial Café, but it helped.

So year after year, the café opened its door to the grieving and down-at-heart. The coffee and tea were always hot and sweet, the small cakes were soft and fresh, and no one noticed how, once a year, something horrible happened there.

Well, Sophie noticed it, but that was to be expected.

On September 9th, 2011, a young lady in her early twenties walked through the door of the café for the first time. She stood momentarily in the doorway, trying to make her eyes adjust to the dimmed light. None of the other customers, three in all, bothered to look up at the new arrival. They were spread out at different tables, nursing half to nearly-empty cups. The young lady took a moment to look around at the dark furnishings, registered the soft, gloomy music playing through the speakers, and finally shut the door behind her.

Gillian Gardner was her name and she had just been visiting someone at Juniper Hill.

She made her way to the front counter and after exchanging a few words with the woman on the other side (who must've weighed two hundred and fifty pounds) ordered a hot drink and went to one of the many empty tables to wait for it.

Before she sat down, she noticed the books.

There were a lot of them; not one of them looked like they'd been moved in less than thirty years.

She let her fingers drift across the spines, dancing languidly from book to book, until something caught her attention.

The woman behind the counter pretended to be involved in nothing more than fixing Gillian's order. Nobody else in the café cared.

She pulled the book from the shelf, hefted it (impressed by its weight), and sat down at a nearby table. Pushing it closer to the dim lamp sitting at the center of the table, she flipped open the cover and started reading.

When she flipped to the second page, she sat back and gasped. The woman behind the counter heard her, realized that the yearly ritual was upon her, and brought over Gillian's coffee. After the two exchanged a few words about what the young girl had read, the café's keeper went back to the counter and resumed her duties of looking busy.

Gillian looked hesitant, as if she might slam the cover shut and leave, forsaking the coffee. If she had looked towards the counter, the woman behind it would've told her with her eyes to get out.

Anything more obvious would've been dangerous.

The young customer shook her head, flipped the page and started reading.

Memorial Tales

Edited by

Hieronymus Scratch

Who does this book belong to? *Jill Gardner*

Will you promise to take care of it? *Yes*

Will you promise to read it all the way through? *Yes*

Good. Turn the page.

READ BY THE LIGHT OF A SINGLE BULB

IT

(1995)
Rebecca Dyne

The sun was going down and the light amongst the trees was dimming, but Bobby walked slowly through the forest, looking apprehensively around yet another tall oak. His hand came away from the bark covered with sap and wiping it on his shirt only succeeded in spreading it. The shadows had elongated since the search started, but Bobby swallowed his fiercely growing fear. He had been against letting it go on after sundown, but of course, he never said anything to the others. A light crackle, like sneakers stepping into dead leaves, had led him to this spot and he opened his eyes wide to absorb what little light was left. Taking care not to step on anything that might scream out his presence, he took a step towards another tree.

Bobby's eyes were so intensely focused on the next tree that he never heard the retreating footsteps, running with a racehorse's speed, until it was too late. He spun around to see a red T-shirt and jeans disappearing into the darkness. Bobby's short legs ran, but he knew that it was too late.

"No Fair," he cried into the trees in front of him, knowing it was completely fair. "No Fair! You can't do that!"

His answer was a fleeting laugh from the figure as it darted away.

"It's not fair," he said to himself as he slowed his pace to a walk.

Trying to fight back a few more frustrated tears, he stepped out from
behind the trees into the clearing. The ones who were waiting for him
started to laugh when he appeared.

All five of them were there, shaking their heads and laughing with
each other as Bobby stumbled into the clearing, his legs sore from
running. Trying not to look too upset, Bobby swallowed hard.

"Looks like Bobby's 'It' again," Chris said, his hand gripping the
tree that they had designated Home, "What's this, the eighth time in a
row?"

"Man, you're gonna be 'It' for the rest of your life," said Bobby's
older brother Charlie, and exchanged a "high-five" with some of the
others.

"Shutup," Bobby said, knowing that he wouldn't be able to hold
on to his frustration for long.

The one named Mike, who always wore a backwards baseball
cap, walked up to him and placed his hand firmly on Bobby's head.
"Whatsamadda', Shrimp" he asked, "can't take it? Wanna run home so
you can start cryin' early or what?"

"Leave me alone," Bobby spat back, shaking himself from
underneath the weight of Mike's hand. He trudged over to the tree,
forcing himself not to cry. He heard Charlie's usual catcall from over his
shoulder.

"You ain't nothin' but a hound dog," Charlie yelled out, to which
the rest of them replied, "*Cryin' all the time!*"

Bobby turned to face the others. All five were staring at him with
wild grins, waiting for Bobby to do anything, no matter how small, that

they could pounce on and laugh about. They were always looking over his shoulders to see what dumb thing he might have said or done lately.

Charlie stepped forward and put his hand on Bobby's shoulder, which made Bobby initially want to pull away just as he did from Mike. Charlie, however, looked him straight in the eyes with only a hint of his original mischievous grin.

"Hey, little man, you want me to be 'It' for a while?"

Charlie's offer was followed immediately by jeers from all the others. The one whose name Bobby could never remember (he had once called him "The Greek" and had gotten a good hard punch in the arm that had bruised up for two weeks) was the first to put in his two cents. "Aw, c'mon Chuck," he said. "Don't let him get away with it! He knows the rules: if he don't catch nobody, he's gotta' be 'It' again."

"Yeah," said the fifth whose name was Myron but everybody called Joe. Joe always shadowed The Greek around and never said much, just kept agreeing with anything everybody else said. Bobby sometimes wondered what Joe did when everyone else went home.

Mike stepped into Bobby's sight. "I guess he's trying to keep the baby from runnin' home with a big load in his diapers..."

"Mike..." Charlie began before he was cut off by Bobby's screaming whine.

"Just *SHUTUP*," he screamed, "I know the rules! I know 'em! You don't have to tell me! I'll be 'It' again!" He abruptly turned and fell against the tree, hiding his eyes in the crook of his arms. Charlie looked at his seven year-old brother and noticed a trembling in his entire body, even though this morning the thermometer had hit ninety-one degrees.

"Scatter," Bobby's muffled voice shouted from his hidden face.

Bobby heard Mike's voice first after the initial scamper of feet.
"C'mon, man! Whatcha' waitin' for?" Charlie's voice, very near,
answered:

"He's been 'It' long enough!"

"Man, that kid was *born* 'It.'"

"Go ahead," Bobby said, and he heard Charlie's sneakers and they
tramped through the leaves to catch up with the others.

Bobby had not started counting; he was crying too hard. Why
can't it be easy, he thought while another part of his brain wondered how
long he could stand here before Mike and the others discovered what he
was really doing. Laboring to keep his loud sobs in his throat, he tried to
start counting again.

"One... Two... Three..." he counted as his mind began to
wander.

I hope you all die!

"Seven... Nine... Ten... Twelve..."

...hope you all go down to Hell and burn there forever...

"Twenty-four...Twenty-nine..."

...To Hell and Kill You...

"Thirty-seven..."

Seeds of vengeful and hideous ideas exploded in his imagination
as he banged his head against the tree to stop the flow of tears. His long
fingernails dug viciously into the tree, digging horrid, winding canals in
the bark. His pointed front teeth bit down and tore away the skin on his
lips, dripping blood down the hair on his chin. His tears were dried up,

killed by the piercing hunger that had taken control of him. Upon opening his eyes, he saw through thin pupils a world that finally was powerless against his seething hatred and yearning hunger.

He turned to the trees that hid Charlie and his friends. Their body heat, as they hid behind the obvious trees and under a few flimsy piles of leaves, burned in his yellow eyes. The smell of their young, warm blood grew fresh and sweet in his nostrils.

"Ready or not, here I come," his cold voice hissed as he waddled into the forest. Saliva dripped from his long tongue as he imagined the fun that awaited him; of seeing The Greek breathe in for the last time before Bobby's claws reached through his neck in search of his windpipe. He would wait on Mike just long enough to see that dark spot appear on the front of his pants. He thought of saving Joe for last, just to see what he could do on his own, but he realized that the final treat was reserved for Charlie. Charlie's head would shake, not believing what eventually came seeking him. He might even turn and run, but he would not get far.

I'm a Hell of a lot more than a hound dog, Bobby thought with hungry lust.

I'm "IT"! Remember me?

IT was finally going to play a game it was going to win.

Brain Food

(2007)
J. Roland Tinzel

The look on the young man's face as he heard the request needed to be seen to be believed. "You wanna *what*?"

"I want to be smarter."

It was almost comical. The one who asked the question was dressed in torn jeans and a black T-shirt that read "My other shirt smells like feet too." The one who answered, who requested intelligence like a kid in a candy store asking for Jawbreakers, was dressed in a dark brown suit. He was in his thirties, slim with slicked back dark brown hair, and the sweat forming on his hairline showed that he was uncomfortable standing at the front door of the young man's apartment. He looked past the young man, saw the posters of hair metal bands on the wall, and then forced himself to look once more at the young man's face, which was pricked with silver studs and pins.

"How'd you find your way here?" the young man asked.

"You mean, who told me about you?" the man in the suit asked back, to which the young man nodded. "Well… a guy hears things… he pieces bits of information together…"

"Give me the easy version," said the young man.

"Mike Remington. He made a comment… more like a joke at a party… not long after his promotion. It was vague, but I caught on.

From there on, I had to ask around, very carefully. I didn't want anyone to think that…"

"I get the idea," the young man said. He looked up into the suited man's face, but was not intimidated by his height. If anything, the man in the suit looked a little like he was on the edge of collapse. "And you thought I could make you smarter?"

"You're the one," the man in the suit said. "I know you can."

The young man closed his mouth and made a face as if he were chewing on his tongue. "Look behind you."

The man in the suit turned and saw the dimly-lit hallway behind him. Opposing doors to the other apartments lined the walls which ended in the stairway that he'd climbed.

"I see it."

"Go back that way and you'll be real smart," said the young man as he slammed the door.

The man in the suit turned back and started pounding on the door with his tightened fists. The pounding echoed down the hallway.

"Open up! You've got to help me! I can pay you! Whatever you want, just open…"

The door was yanked open again and the young man stood there, his mouth curled in impatience.

"What the Hell are you doing, Man? You keep this up and I'll call the cops!"

"You'd do that?" the man in the suit asked. "There are rumors about you, you know… about how you do what you do. I've heard about what you have in there; you wouldn't want the police to come in there, would you?"

The young man just stood in his doorway, his expression unchanging.

"I said I would pay you. I've got the kind of money you need."

"What kind of money do I need?" the young man asked.

The man in the suit took a deep breath before answering. "Enough to move somewhere else. That's what you do after a job, right? Relocate? That's why it's so hard to find you. You pick up and move as soon as the job is..."

The young man stepped aside. The man in the suit took a moment to look around him and, seeing that no one was looking, stepped inside.

* * *

Jeremy Van Dyke certainly didn't consider himself stupid by any stretch of the imagination. Indeed, he'd been a good student, graduated with high honors as a Communications major from Florida State and had landed a good job at Millburn Genesis Inc. a decade and change before and things were going fine in the strictest sense of the word. As an assistant to Mr. Dennings, the assistant head of Public Relations, he'd made a good living. His wife and son were completely content in their small home in Boston and they seemed perfectly fine with Jeremy's plan to save up for another five years before they could put a down payment on a bigger one. And there had been nothing to disturb Jeremy's piece of mind in his current situation: Ginny was perfectly content to work as a tax consultant from home while keeping an eye on their little wonder

Tony who, at the budding age of six, was already showing signs of a remarkable intelligence that had to have come from his mother's side of the genes. He was watching Mommy work over her shoulder just as much as he was watching cartoons and he seemed to understand the process by which a long column of numbers became a sum. No, nothing had been bothering Jeremy about the job that he was proficient at and the two faces that greeted him when he got home.

At least that had been the case up until about eighteen months ago. When Remington had leapfrogged into the top position in the PR department, everything changed.

Not right away, of course. At first, Jeremy had only been mildly annoyed that Remington, who had joined the department only six months before and showed only a reasonable amount of brains and aptitude, suddenly bloomed into the wonderboy that everyone had been waiting for just at the moment when they needed him, when the original department head, Ms. Carlson, had suddenly resigned without warning. Yes, that'd been annoying, especially when Remington insisted that Jeremy add the word "Mister" to Remington's name whenever he addressed him. Jeremy had chewed his lip, narrowed his eyes, and bowed his head back down to the computer screen to get back to work.

"Well," he'd muttered when Remington's promotion was first announced, "I guess he knows something I don't."

Just a thought, nothing more… but a thought that wouldn't go anyway.

At night when Ginny was sleeping peacefully beside him, he sometimes found himself staring into the dark, confused. At first he believed he was thinking of nothing at all: so many thoughts passed through his head at such speed that it was almost like thinking of nothing at all. He'd turn up at work, more often than not, groggy and a bit dazed. His work didn't suffer, but soft voices whispered about him, about the change in his demeanor, his temperament, and about what might be causing it. After a board meeting, Remington (*MISTER* Remington... *MISTER* Remington) had asked him to stay behind for a few minutes.

"Van Dyke, I've been meaning to ask you," he'd said before pausing to choose his words. "...are you happy here?"

The question had taken Jeremy by surprise. "M-Mr. Remington, I can't see why you'd feel the need to ask me that. I've been here for more than ten years and I'm very proud at what I've been able to achieve as a member of this team."

Remington had leaned back in his chair, his fingers steepled in front of his mouth as if in prayer, although his eyes had never stopped looking at Jeremy.

"The team isn't exactly the same as it was when you first joined, is it?"

Jeremy hadn't been sure what to make of this. "Uh... I suppose not."

Remington had responded almost absently. "Teams are always changing, aren't they? The Red Sox, for example: Carl Yastremski... Jim Rice... but neither of them were on the team when they won the World Series..."

"I'm committed to the team, Mr. Remington."

Remington had taken a moment to lean further back, stare at the ceiling and finally grunt and dismiss Jeremy with a wave of his hand.

That night, all Jeremy could see when he closed his eyes was that waving hand, shooing him like a fly.

Life continued, projects got accomplished at MGI, Jeremy pulled his weight and got the occasional pat on the shoulder for his efforts. His innards still simmered and at least seventy minutes of sleep were sacrificed while staring at the darkness above his bed, wondering what had gone so horribly wrong.

And then came the company Christmas party, when liquor flowed and old corporate wounds were exacerbated on the tidal breath of booze, all in good fun, of course. At some point in the evening, Mike Remington had found his way to Jeremy's side and had to use his shoulder briefly to steady himself. More than blood was flowing through his veins.

"Having a good time?" Remington had asked.

"A very good time." Not much of a lie; Jeremy had had a few drinks himself and had been entering the realm of smooth drunkenness that he always strived for: a magical place between stone-sober and shit-faced where music drifted like a fresh breeze through his ears and the world tilted into just the right position to fit his disposition. At least, that had been the case until Remington had sidled up to him with all the grace of an elephant on a banana skin.

"You know that you're a huge part of the team, right?"

"Yes, Mr. Remington." Even in his drunken state, he couldn't bring himself to call him "Sir."

"You're going to be a legend on the day you retire. I can see the plaque on the wall of the foyer in years to come: 'Jeremy Van Dyke – the strength and backbone of MGI.'"

Jeremy nodded and tried his best not to bring up the question of his pay scale for one who would be so honored in future times. Then Remington had said something that seemed to make no sense.

"But not the stomach. Not strong enough."

"Excuse me?"

Remington had looked at him with a sloppy smile and awkwardly brought his mouth to Jeremy's ear.

"You need a stronger stomach, Van Dyke. Decide what you want out of life, find those things… and *eat* them! Just like a hamburger or steak: it can all be yours if you can get your teeth around it. It's not as bad as you think… Ms. Carlson…"

And Jeremy had found himself sobering, but had no idea why: something was telling him that this was the most important thing that he was likely to hear in his life. He trained what little sense he had at the gin-fumed mouth beside him. "What about Ms. Carlson?"

"Well…" Remington had swayed a bit, trying to focus his thoughts. When he did, Jeremy had seen his boss's shoulders hunch as if something at the base of his spine had frozen him from saying more. Jeremy looked intently into Remington's eyes and could read volumes of secrets hidden within his pupils.

"Just… just apply yourself," Remington said in a voice that no longer sounded commanding. He pushed himself away from Jeremy and, with an air of almost shrinking shame, made his way to the bar to refresh his martini glass.

The music continued, laughter reigned, men tickled their dancing partners' ribs to get a kiss, and Jeremy stood where he'd planted himself, thinking about what Remington had said.

Find those things… and eat them… get your teeth around it…

* * *

"First of all, have you got anyone at home waiting for you?"

Jeremy wasn't prepared for personal questions and the last person he wanted to confide in was a kid with piercings in his face. "I have a family, yeah."

"Call your wife and tell her that you're going to be late. Once I start, I can't stop. You understand?"

Jeremy nodded. The kid leaned forward and looked into Jeremy's eyes.

"Answer me: do you understand what I've just told you?"

"Y-Yes…"

"There's no going back. Once it begins, you're committed. Don't even think about trying to find me again; I'm good at disappearing. There's no 'Satisfaction Guaranteed' with me. I do what I do and that's it. Now, do you understand?"

If he had been standing against a wall, Jeremy would've felt nailed to it by the kid's words and stare. Instead, he sat with his back pressed tightly against the back of one of the kitchen table chairs. There was a force to the kid's stare, something that started to make his eyes water.

"I understand."

The kid looked at him. "You want to be smarter?"

"Yes."

"Nothing comes from nothing."

Jeremy was lost again; the look on his face said so.

"I can't create anything," the kid said. "I can take from one and put it in another. The power is unstable: I don't control it. It seeps..."

Jeremy wasn't sure what to make of what he was hearing. He could see that the kid couldn't either: he shook his head to clear it.

"It'll give you what you ask for, but at the cost of someone else. I can't change that. Sometimes it even plays..." The kid fell silent for a moment. "I can't control it, understand?"

"I understand."

"How smart do you want to be?"

"I want it all."

The kid leaned back in his chair and took a deep breath. "Call your wife."

"When does it start?"

"It just did."

* * *

For the first twenty minutes, he had to endure the kid's hands in his hair. Not a word was said as the kid placed his clamp-like fingers on his scalp and gripped it tight. There were no charms or invocations: simply the slow, controlled breath of the kid and he pressed deeper into Jeremy's head. Finally, the kid broke his grip and stood in front of him with his arms splayed out. His cheeks tightened, his left hand wavered in the air and Jeremy thought he was about to have a seizure. Instead, he backed away from his client and started for the kitchen with a tired and staggering walk. Just before he disappeared into the kitchen, he said in a choked voice:

"There are DVDs. Watch what you like."

The kid was gone and Jeremy was left alone. He looked towards the TV and saw a large shelf of DVDs standing next to it.

He chose *Goodfellas*.

Robert DeNiro and Ray Liotta were just about to feed some poor schmuck to the lions when the kid came out of the kitchen with a plate in his hands.

"It's ready."

He laid the plate on the table and stepped backwards as if removing himself from the radius of destruction. The bare bulb above the table shone on a brown slab of cooked meat, freshly out of the oven. There was no flair like the chefs on TV do as they presented the prefect meal that they'd been promising for the past thirty minutes; the lump of meat on the plate was small, not much bigger than two hands clamped tightly together, brown and nearly pulsating with its bubbling juices. Jeremy approached the table with trepidation.

"What's that?"

The kid bit his lip before answering. "That is the brain of the most intelligent person alive today on the planet. That's what you requested: don't deny it because my fingers never lead me astray."

Jeremy took another look at it and sneered: it was quite obviously a smallish, slightly undercooked meatloaf. "You've got to be kidding me."

"What did you think I was going to bring you, an actual brain?"

"You want me to pay you for this?"

"In cash." The kid didn't flinch; there was nothing in his look or tone that gave away any possibility that this was one gigantic joke. In fact, he'd raised an eyebrow as if he was proud of his medium-rare masterpiece.

Jeremy still wasn't convinced. "You know, for all your 'Once I start, I can't stop' stuff, you made a big mistake: I've yet to pay you. What's to stop me from walking out of here without eating that thing?"

"Nothing." Again, no sign of hesitation or worry.

Jeremy sighed. "How much did Remington pay you to set me up?"

"Mr. Van Dyke, nothing is stopping you from leaving without your meal, but what I said earlier holds true: I started this and it can not be stopped. The thoughts and ideas of the smartest person in the world are sitting on that plate and there they will stay. They're not going back to their original home: that's completely beyond me. Someone in this world has suddenly found all of his or her genius wiped completely away and are probably blinking into the nearest light bulb, wondering what it does. You can either leave what is on that plate sitting there or you can eat it. But you won't take a bite until I get paid."

Jeremy looked at the lump of meat again.

"You came all this way based on just weird rumors," the kid said. "And *now* you're coming to your senses? Someone has already suffered because of you, Mr. Van Dyke; the next step is up to you."

There could be anything in that… bottles of arsenic, toilet-bowl cleaner, dolphin flesh…

"Your future is getting cold, Mr. Van Dyke."

Maybe it's Remington's brain…

He paid the kid and started eating.

* * *

"So you finally made it home, huh? I've been keeping your supper warm so… Honey, what is it?"

Ginny had noticed something strange about her husband as he crossed from the door to the kitchen table and grabbed hold of a chair to steady himself: he was breathing heavily and sweating and, while the coloring of his face didn't look any paler than normal, she had felt certain that, for an instant, the chair was the only thing keeping him standing. She went to him and grabbed his shoulders. "Honey, are you alright?"

After taking a deep breath, Jeremy's eyes open wider and the glazed look passed. He wiped his brow and focused on her. "Gin, I'm okay. Someone sent out for KFC and… I know how greasy it is but…"

"Oh Jem, you knew that I was going have something *decent* for you to eat when you got home; you didn't have to go snacking on that stuff." She gave him a big hug that threatened to make him gag, but it had nothing to do with his stomach. True, he hadn't felt entirely well while he was eating the meatloaf: undercooked was a polite way of describing it, but the kid had claimed that to cook it properly would "cremate the cells" and that didn't sound good at all. He'd sat at the kid's table an extra twenty-two minutes, hyperventilating and fighting the gorge that wanted nothing more than to shoot back out from where it had come in. The kid had kept him at the kitchen table (and eventually, *under* the kitchen table), telling him over and over again that someone in the world had just lost their mind and he was not about to vomit all that knowledge and genius on the carpet. So Jeremy had struggled, swallowed every time he'd felt the impulse to do the opposite, and pounded the floor until the wave of nausea had finally passed.

It was the other feeling that had caused the dizziness: the feeling in his head.

Like buds blossoming… ideas… from the most basic concepts of science that escaped me when I was in high school… quantum physics… the new possibilities of energy in the twenty-first century… I can see it unfolding in my head… I can see it all… Public Relations at MGI is nothing… it all makes sense to me now…

"Jem?" Ginny searched his face and knew that there was something he wasn't telling her, but she was grateful when she felt the strength surge back into his body.

"I'm okay, Gin; I promise. In fact, I'm feeling much better than I have in a long time." He took another deep breath. "Yes, this is much better than I ever thought…"

"What? What are you talking about?" Despite his words, Ginny still looked worried; it wasn't just woman's intuition that told her that something had drastically changed her husband, no matter if it was for good or for ill.

Jeremy took control of his hands, which previously had been shaking with the excitement of all the new incredible notions in his head, and ran them soothingly down her arms. "Everything's good,

Sweetheart. In fact, I can safely say that things are going to be much better from this point forward."

Ginny was calmed by his strong hands but still confused by his words. "What? Jem, I don't think I under…"

"You don't have to," he said with a big smile. "You remember how we wanted to get a house bigger than this old matchstick shack?"

"Jem, you shouldn't say things like that; it's cozy enough for me…"

"…you're gonna have more than enough space for your clothes; trust me! Something happened tonight that opened up more doors of opportunity than you can imagine. Think about having servants, Ginny: you won't have to warm up leftovers for me anymore! I can finally give you the things you deserve!"

She placed her hands on either side of his face and felt the blood pumping furiously through his veins. "Jem, calm down! What happened tonight?"

At that moment, his blood pressure slowed and his excitement was replaced by a complete feeling of bliss. "I… I just know that… things are going to get better for the three of us from now on. And who knows: maybe four or five of us wouldn't be out of the question."

Ginny, who had been secretly hoping that she might be blessed by more than one child in her lifetime, clasped her fingers together for a moment before she launched herself onto her husband and kissed him all over his face. Jeremy could barely stop laughing.

"I love you too, Honey," he said. "This is a big day for all of us, Tony too. Where is he?"

"He's in the living room, watching TV."

"I'll go get him. Throw away whatever you've been warming up and I'll take you both out for the greatest meal you've ever had!"

"But we've eaten already…"

"It's a celebration! One more meal won't hurt."

Ginny couldn't find a reason to argue with him, his enthusiasm was too strong to combat. "Just give me some time to get ready," she said before happily running for the bedroom to change into proper celebration clothes. At the sound of her ecstatic squeak, Jeremy breathed in one more deep lungful of satisfaction before turning towards the living room, from which he could hear cartoons playing. He knew that Tony, as smart as he was, wouldn't completely understand his father's joy at all the new ideas in his head and how he could turn them into a better life for his family. He'd just grab his son by the shoulders and shake him gently as he always did when he had a surprise for him. And oh… what a surprise!

The galaxy is opening before me… space travel is clay in my hands… light speed is nowhere near fast enough for me!

Jeremy went into the living room and saw Tony sitting there, with his back towards him, watching the television: frenetic cartoons were playing in front of him at top speed – all speed and few laughs. It had been a while since Jeremy had sat down with his son to watch evening cartoons, but he could still remember a time not too long before when Tony was watching programs that had a few more laughs than what he was currently watching. He was also sitting on the floor, much closer to the TV than he usually did. Jeremy was in too good a mood to consider any of this: he shrugged and immediately crouched down to the floor to meet up with his son.

"Hey Tiger," he said, "Daddy's finally home and he is taking you and Mommy out for a good time! And it won't be the first time, let me tell you. You think you can tear yourself away from Cartoon Network for a while?"

Tony continued watching TV; he didn't acknowledge his father's presence so close to his right ear.

"Tiger, we can tape this. You can watch it later. Your Dad's just done something extraordinary. You might not understand it now, but…"

Tony still didn't budge; he kept his head steadfast and sturdy towards the TV. Jeremy stretched his head around to look into Tony's face.

"Tony…"

Tony, who was six years old, was doing something that he hadn't done since before his first birthday: drooling.

Profusely.

His shirt and the floor in front of him was drenched in his slobs. His tongue was protruding just over his loose and slobbering lower lip. Jeremy, who had never been comfortable with his son during his first year when he had done nothing but spew gooey gunk at a moment's notice, felt the gorge that he had been trying to keep at bay only an hour before starting to rise again.

He swallowed, looked down and felt even sicker.

The carpet on which his son was sitting on was stained with more than just drool: familiar odors began rising up and striking old memories. He looked down and found himself recognizing a brown mush seeping out of the edges of Tony's shorts; yellow liquid that he knew was urine trickled through the fibers of the fabric. And through it all, Tony never wavered his gaze away from the television set.

"Tony? Tony are you al…"

And then he remembered.

… the most intelligent person alive today on the planet…

A horrible thought came to the father of the incontinent child watching cartoons.

The most intelligent person… could that apply to the most intelligent person… YET TO COME?

Tony was a smart kid, had always been a smart kid: he'd learned to read a year before the books said he was expected to, he'd counted up past one hundred and understood the concept of numbers rolling over to the next digit long before any of the other children in his class, and he not only grasped but was interested in what his mother was calculating every time she bent over a tax form.

And he was only six years old. What could he possibly have been capable of at sixteen… or twenty-four…

Tony…

Jeremy looked at his drooling, incontinent son who had, only the day before, been reducing complex fractions without any help from his parents. He reached forward and squeezed his brainless son to his chest, provoking a new stream of snot to spew forth and run down his suit while thinking all the thoughts that his son, given time, would've been thinking throughout the rest of his life if given the chance that all other children had. The idiot's father wept as he rocked his son back and forth.

"Jeremy," Ginny called from the bedroom, "have you gotten Tony ready?"

For all his new-found intelligence, Jeremy Van Dyke had no clue what to say.

The Damned Queen

(1975)
Dame Veronica Tremble

O nce upon a time in a shadowy kingdom on the other side of the Deep Pit of Terror lay a castle that housed a King and Queen who wanted to remain young forever. To this end, the kingdom's most advanced sages and alchemists researched the grave problem that was set in front of them, but they always balked at a certain formula that existed at the back of the largest tome housed in the darkest and dustiest section of the great library. None dared to mention it to the royals because none dared to dangle the prize in front of their eyes… not for the cost of the terrible recipe.

And so, time went on and failure after failure met with the King and Queen until one day when, in a fit of temper, the King had his chief sage tortured. The King was simply impatient and was taking his frustrations out on the poor man, so he was completely caught by surprise when the old sage blurted out the existence of the terrible recipe.

The King and Queen hurried into the great library, despite the protestations of all their alchemists and sages, and found the tome. They looked in the back of the book and found what they were looking for.

The recipe was vague and there would need to be some experiments conducted, but one ingredient was plainly clear.

Children

The alchemists and sages fled from the castle, wanting no part of the experiment. The oldest and wisest sage, who had blurted out the secret while secured tightly to the rack, screeched, "Satan will find you! You must not take part in the madness! He will find you!" The King and Queen took turns tightening the great wheel on the rack until the old sage said nothing more.

Two nights later, a young village girl named Victoria disappeared. No one knew how it happened, but it did happen.

And it happened again... and again.

The old sage's words took root in the royal couple. Fearing that Satan would indeed find them and punish them, they stopped calling each other by name. Their fear stemmed from their belief that the devil used his pointed and shiny horns as extra auditory senses, leaving him with the most extraordinary sense of hearing.

"He'll hear us as we work," the King said in hushed tones that he somehow knew were never hushed enough. "We must find a way to keep him at bay."

"There are voices enough from all over the world," his wife answered, pressing her lips close to his ear so that she could be heard. "Surely the noise must be gobbledygook to his four ears. As long as we do not ever address each other by name, we might find a way of talking and planning without him catching on to us. Let us forget our names. We can surely trick the Lord Of The Flies. He'll not find us, I swear."

And so it came to pass that a proclamation was carried forth into the kingdom that the King and Queen's names were never to be uttered, upon pain of a most unpleasant death. The subjects of the monarchs heeded the proclamation with great sincerity and fear because rumors had spread of the wild experiments taking place beneath the floor of the Great Hall in the castle. With every child that disappeared, the rumors grew and grew until the blackest of all black clouds seemed to hang motionless over the kingdom. So black and thick was the cloud that day and night seemed to disappear from both the lives and vocabulary of the kingdom.

The peasants in the village that rested at the foot of the great castle went about their days and mumbled to themselves.

And their children disappeared.

And so time went on and the clouds became darker over the village and children would disappear sometimes and every once in a while an adult would be arrested for muttering the King or Queen's name in public. These adults were often turned in by parents hoping to have their children returned in appreciation for keeping the new law sacred, but none of the children ever returned.

Through it all, the King and Queen knew better than to leave the confines of their castle. The ugliness brewed, the air got thicker and staler and it wafted into the castle under the monarchs' noses and reminded them of their sins so they would retreat deeper and deeper into the confines of the castle to escape the smell. Rarely did they greet visitors in the Great Hall as they were too afraid of the stench that drifted in and out with the wind (and to tell the truth, few visitors could stand the air any better than the royals did).

And then one day, on the first day of the year, a visitor came calling.

Guards stationed at the drawbridge, their noses clipped tightly shut with clumsy, hand-fashioned clips of wood, were surprised one morning to hear a voice calling to them from the other side of the moat.

"Lower the drawbridge! Raise the portcullis! Welcome the King!"

Now the guards knew that the King, along with his wife, was safely locked up in one of the laboratories located beneath the Great Hall. Their fine bedroom abandoned, the royal couple spent their nights on rough and foul cots hauled into the laboratories so that they would not breathe the sullen air and be reminded of how monstrous they had become. The Captain of the Guards peered out through the narrow arrow loop to see who was really at the heart of this matter.

To the experienced eyes of the Captain, the stranger was obviously no king. His thin body was swathed in several robes that criss-crossed his chest. His long hair was white and his beard reached to nearly his waist. Despite the look of age and wisdom that his clothes and hair lent him, his face looked remarkably young and unlined. In fact, except for the youthfulness of his face, the Captain was reminded of the old sage who had been stretched by the King and Queen years before.

His fine, booming voice bellowed the same command as before. "Lower the drawbridge! Raise the portcullis! Welcome the King!"

In the stranger's hands was a box covered with a velvet cloth. He held it out proudly like a calling card.

"Lower the drawbridge! Raise the portcullis! Welcome the King!"

Sentries were dispatched (through a draw of lots as few wanted to disturb the royal couple) to the bowels of the castle. Nervously, they knocked upon the door that they knew the King and Queen were sure to be behind.

At that very moment, the King and Queen were involved in a very delicate procedure involving a three year-old girl's eyeball when they were both startled by the knock upon the door. The eyeball flew from the Queen's tray and was lost.

The King wasted no time in venting his displeasure. "Who disturbs us at this moment? A night's worth of work completely ruined by you swines! I promise you that if someone isn't dead, *someone is going to be!*"

"Sire, a stranger has come to the front gates. He calls himself a king and demands to be allowed access."

"And is he a king?" the King asked.

"He looks more like a sage than a king, but speaks like a great monarch and he has a gift for you."

"Does he?" This was the Queen who answered, whose womanly pleasure at receiving gifts was aroused after a long sleep. "By all means, allow him access. We will meet him in the Great Hall."

"The Great Hall?" The thought of returning to the choking atmosphere of the upper-level filled the once-brave King with shakes and shivers.

"Would you rather that we receive him here in this room with that… thing laying there?" The Queen's head motioned towards the tiny body lying on the examination table.

"But what of the air? You know how much it displeases me."

"No more so than I, dear husband, but we will receive him only long enough to find his purpose and receive his gift. He is no king, for no king will travel on foot dressed as a sage. We will bid him gone as soon as the gift is passed over and, if he refuses to go, we'll stretch him like the last sage."

The king smirked at the thought and gave the order to the two frightened guards to allow the stranger admittance.

With that, the King and Queen each retired to their chambers that lay along the same hall as the laboratory. Each splashed water onto their faces, each pinched their cheeks to bring color back to them, and each secreted a dagger under the folds of their garments.

You see, as their sins grew greater and greater without the consolation of a successful experiment, the two had begun to blame each other for their continual failure and for the ever growing number of lives that stained their souls to an ever-worsening degree. Frustration had turned to mistrust, mistrust to reproaches, reproaches to full arguments...

... and arguments to plots.

Ignoring their faded clothes and dusty, scratched ornaments, the damned royal couple made their way, arm-in-arm, to the Great Hall. Almost immediately, the smell of the air staggered the King and the Queen pressed her handkerchief tightly to her nose to deaden the sound of a snuffle. Both of them nearly turned and ran back to the haven of their laboratory but neither of them wanted to be seen as a coward in the eyes of the other. So, with eyes watering, noses running and lungs threatening to hack, the royal couple took their places on the thrones of the Great Hall.

The doors opened and in walked the stranger. As the cowardly sentry had described, he was dressed as a sage and was holding out in front of him a box covered in velvet. Despite the mutiny of their senses caused by the air, the King and Queen both found themselves drawn towards the stranger's hands and the hidden gift. The very air that they dreaded to breathe seemed to flow lighter through their lungs as the stranger came closer.

"Welcome the King," the stranger said as he reached the dais.

"I *am* the King. What is it you have there?"

"A gift, your Royal Highnesses." The stranger held the box even closer to the royal couple. They both took a moment to look at each other and grin before turning their attention back to the stranger.

"Let us look upon it," said the Queen.

"I'm afraid I have only one gift and it must go to the most deserving of you."

At this, the King sat back and huffed impatiently. Through his mind flew the ten most enjoyable ways that he could end this impertinent stranger's life.

"How dare you qualify a King against his own wife! What makes you think that woman is more deserving of any gift than I am?"

The stranger smiled and lowered his eyes before the angered monarch. The Queen saw something in the smile she didn't like.

"If you'll forgive me, Your Highness, but the criteria to receive this particular gift is old and sacred and, while I find you both nearly equally worthy, there is a quality in the makeup of Her Majesty's heart that may put her in the lead."

"Oh really?" the King asked. "And what quality is that, foolish sage?"

The stranger raised his eyes again to the monarch.

"Her capacity for cruelty is slightly keener than yours, Sire. After all, was it not her hand that plucked the eye from the living child last night?"

And with that, both the King and Queen gasped in shock on their thrones. The King stood up and took three steps towards the stranger, trembling.

"Whatever you have, I don't want it! You're right; she's the one! She plucked the eye, just as you say! It was her vanity that started us on this path in the first place! Whatever it is, give it to her! To her! To Queen J..."

And as the first syllable of the Queen's name, which her husband had sworn never to reveal, passed his lips, his throat was pierced by the dagger that his wife had secreted.

The King fell to the floor of the Great Hall. The Queen marched from the place where she'd thrown the dagger and pulled the weapon from her husband's throat, wiping the blood on her dress.

"And now, sage," she said, "I know not where you came to know the things you know, but I'll have your source by sundown. As your source most probably told you, we have a great many devices below which has made even the most tight-lipped sing, so if you be..."

But when the Queen looked up from her husband's corpse, she saw that the stranger had gone.

Only the box remained, now sitting on the floor.

The Queen crept up to the box, afraid but not wanting to show it, even though she was the only living person in the Great Hall. Using the point of her dagger, she caught the corner of the velvet and flipped it aside.

After looking for a moment, the Queen squealed with joy.

Within the box was a crown.

Even with so little light to illuminate the Great Hall, the Queen could plainly see the glittering object within. Fascinated, she dropped her dagger and took the crown from the box, holding it up to the window so that she could see it better.

The crown was made of gold and was encrusted with jewels. Her eyes were dazzled by the sight. It was cold to the touch, but inviting at the same time. So enraptured was she by the crown that she nearly didn't notice the parchment attached by a golden thread. She took the parchment in hand and peered at what was written there.

This will give you what you sought.

In a moment, she knew exactly what the crown could do. Wasting no more time, she tore the parchment from the crown, threw it aside and placed the crown gingerly on her head.

Almost immediately, the Queen felt a ripple of fire go through her. It did not pain her, but instead made the hairs on her body alive. Excited, she ran from the Great Hall and made her way down to her chamber below to find the looking glass.

There, in the looking glass, was the face of a woman thirty years younger looking back her.

Her face… her *young* face…

The Queen jumped with joy and danced about her chamber,

kicking aside whatever furniture could be moved by the force of her foot. She howled in amazement and sang until her voice reverberated all over the castle.

"I'm young," she sang. "I'm young, young, young, young, YOUNG!!!!!!"

The experiments stopped that day. No more children disappeared and the black clouds of bereavement slowly drifted away to find another cursed place. Although the villagers were still saddened by the loss of their children, they eventually began to get on with their lives.

The Queen, meanwhile, feared to take the mighty magical crown off in dread that her former countenance would return. So she continued to wear it, even going so far as to sleep sitting up so the crown would not slip off. It was uncomfortable, but she was determined to keep the crown on her head.

And then the heat began.

One day the crown began to burn the skin on her head. Smoke rose from her scalp. The hair around the crown burned away. She screamed and ordered her servants to pour water on her head, but to no avail. The crown continued to burn her.

Soon her head was scalded red and blisters formed around the crown, suppurating and dribbling only long enough for new ones to form. She screamed and cried, but the burning continued. Her servants fled her side, screaming that she was bewitched. The guards followed suit soon after, leaving her alone in the moldering castle as she screamed her throat into rupture.

And never once did she take the crown from her head.

She could not face the looking glass and see the old woman she formally was. No, this was better, she decided. So every day, she stood before the looking glass, tears streaming down her face and admiring her beautiful eyes and mouth, being careful to ignore the hideousness that was the top of her head.

Never did she take the crown from her head, even when she happened across the parchment that she had thrown aside so long before when she first received the crown. She'd been moaning in agony, making her way through the Great Hall when the dusty parchment, lying near her old throne, caught her eye. She flew to it and scooped it up, meaning to tear it to pieces in misplaced anger, when she noticed for the first time that something was written on the back.

To Queen J, Live forever as you wished.

She'd only heard herself called that once.

It was her husband's last words.

The stranger had no time to write that on the parchment before he disappeared.

The stranger had called himself a King.

The Queen now knew this to be true.

Outside the castle, the children who had survived her murderous plot grew up and had children of their own, who in turn had children of *their* own. After a time, no one survived who personally remembered the King and Queen and the disappearing children. Children would look up at the great, shambled castle and ask their fathers who lived there and their fathers would relate the old folk tale about the evil royal couple who got a visit from a stranger bearing a gift; a gift that gave one of them exactly what they wanted.

And when a child grew fearful of the strange, agonized moaning that floated from the castle from time to time, what would his father say?

"It's just the wind, my son. Did you really think that the story was true?"

Broken Record

(2001)
Raymond Taylor-Hogg

I swear that I never saw the man's face before I killed him; if I had, I never would have fired.

The house is isolated so no one came running at the sound of the gunshot and no birds flew panicked into the sky like they do in movies. I can't even remember if the air around me moved. It was cold, that I *do* remember; I never liked the cold and standing in front of a dead man wasn't making the cold any better. I took a step forward and faltered; just a moment before the bullet pierced his forehead, he was standing with his hand out in front of him and shouting his last three words "No, you mustn't..." in a strangled voice. I didn't register those words at the time; all I could think of was the need to be rid of him once and for all. He was shaking and crying as he spoke his last, as if he could see by the look in my eyes that he was a goner. That's what I thought at the time. Now I know better.

Although this may sound like the memoirs of a mafia hitman, a drug dealer or a Southern Republican, you'll know that that's not the truth. It was the first time I'd ever fired my father's service pistol, just out of its case for the first time in ten years, or any other gun for that matter and it now lies on top of the dead man in the shallow grave I dug for him in the woods on the back edge of my property. That may sound like a safe place for it, but now I'm beginning to wonder.

I am Professor Hunter Westlake and, unless I am very careful, the gun will be used again.

This began as a series of self-funded experiments at the house that used to belong to my father. My father made his career in the military and rose to the Joint Chiefs of Staff in 1987. He somehow managed to exemplify that most rare of creatures: the officer who treated his troops like his troops and his son like his son. Not once, from the beginning of my life to the end of his, did he come home like The Great Santini and demand an inspection of my personal latrine. My bedtime as a child was 9:00 pm, not 2100 hours. And the only thing that he pushed me into being was whatever I wanted to be. Don't ask me how he did it - even science can't explain it -

but the day he died of a heart attack in his sleep at the age of 72, I ceased asking "how can it be" and began asking "why can't it be."

A voracious appetite for science fiction as a child led to a more mature interest in science as High School faded into the distance. Unlike many who are disappointed to discover that science is not just pressing a button and zipping around the stars, I was more intrigued by the reality of it all, but not because I'm some myopic science-geek whose only interest is subatomic particles in a petrie dish (my eyesight, in fact, is 20/20). It was because I, alone of all the students, faculty and colleagues I've been associated with, was the only one to see the true and real connection between the stories of Jack Finney and the laws of physics. I alone saw that there was no real disconnect between space fiction and reality because the laws of reality were incomplete, because the whole history of astrophysics had been dictated by one-eyed explorers leading the blind to their accepted half-truths such as the nature of light and the direction of time. One (*this* one, I hasten to add) needed only to see the concepts connected as no other scientist had connected them before: Thermal and Black-Body radiation, starlight, measurements from Foot-candles to Kelvin, the Space-time Continuum and elements as simple as lines of binary numbers commanding yes or no at the precise moments. My first reward was scoffs and eye rolls, progressing slowly to patient silence, distance and finally professional shunning. Even my father, in the last of his vibrant months of life, expressed only half-hearted praise at my theoretical success. That's what hurt the most: the wisest and kindest man in my life hedging his enthusiasm on my discoveries. At the time, I tried to persuade myself that it was age and illness dictating him. I now realize that was not the case: I now realize that I should have listened.

After his death and after the inheritance and property were legally mine, I wasted no time in building a device that would fulfill the sum-total of all my work. There is no need to go into details: there's no time. Seconds of inspiration led to years of work as I developed the device. At the end of seven years, the completed mechanism loomed in front of me in what was once the third-floor master bedroom, the largest room in the house. I had long before retreated to the room of my childhood during those few minutes when I desired sleep, but being wide awake, I looked in awe at the machine that would prove to all that I could see further into the microcosm of science than any who had come before me.

On October 24th, 2001 , I would travel in time.

On that day, I stripped bare and stepped into the suit I'd designed to protect me from the rays that would have otherwise scorched me once I'd entered the first doorway. Once safely inside the suit and peering through the heavily-tinted visor, I engaged the remote strapped to my wrist and looked into the first doorway. The doorway lit up with an impossibly-bright light that should have roasted my eyes had I not been wearing the visor. With its help, I could see not only the doorway, but the corridor that lay beyond it. The corridor, arched and made of dense lead, was only two feet and three and one-quarter inches long before it ended in the second doorway (as my precise calculations dictated), but it pulsated with the intense light. Each L.E.D. on the console flashed in the exact pattern that I'd memorized four years before for the first time. I'd set the coordinates for something simple for the initial run: sixty minutes into the past, from 11:16 pm to 10:16 pm. I'd hung a clock at the far end of the room in front of the second doorway; I couldn't see it from my starting point, but it would be the first thing I saw as I emerged. Each buckle and clasp on the suit was secured to protect me; I was ready. Taking a deep breath, I stepped through.

My foot didn't hit solid ground at the moment I thought it

should; it took an extra second. Once I'd landed, I could see the clock

in front of me.

11:16.

I blinked, used the remote to turn the device off and, once the

doors sealed and my suit's Geiger counter dipped back into the realm

of safety, ripped off the visor to make sure I'd seen it correctly.

Sixteen minutes and forty-seven seconds past the twenty-

third hour of the day.

I was shocked: everything was working at the exact level that

I'd calculated. It should have sent me back one hour into the past;

the clock should've read 10:16. It should have but didn't. I ripped

off the protective suit as quickly as my shaking hands could, stepped

out of it and kicked it away. I must've made quite a sight, standing

in front of my would-be masterpiece, naked, sweating, and resisting

the urge to tear my hair out. I let out a roar of frustration.

Once that was out of me, an odd feeling came over me:

maybe it was because I was naked, but I suddenly felt as if I were

being watched.

I first looked to the door and then to the several windows

lining the room. I'd felt no need to board them up or even draw the

curtains on them before the experiment: the estate was not only isolated but also guarded by electric fencing. I never imagined that there could be somebody peering at me and, more importantly, the device. But that's exactly what was happening at the eastern window. Fog had drifted in and obscured the face from clear viewing, but it was there: the open mouth was all I could clearly see.

Before even thinking about covering myself, I grabbed a marble ashtray and heaved it at the window. The face ducked down just before the window smashed. I could hear the intruder gasping as he hurriedly climbed down what I could now see was a ladder propped up against the windowsill. I took the safety suit and threw it over whatever shards of broken glass had fallen inwards so I could get to the window. A jagged piece of the pane scratched my right cheek and drew blood as I stuck my head out, but I barely felt it; all I wanted was a clear look at who had infiltrated the grounds. The fog worked against me: all I saw three floors down was a man in a gray sweatshirt stumbling on the last few rungs and falling to the ground. He wasn't prostrate for even five seconds before he scrambled up, muttering "Jesus... Jesus..." before disappearing into the fog.

Instinct took over as I scrambled to put on whatever clothes were lying around and ran downstairs to see the control panel for the alarm system in the main foyer; for the life of me, I can't

remember searching for and finding the gun. I got to the panel and

stared at the L.E.D.-studded map, so worked up that I literally had

to keep looking at it for almost a minute before I could take in

anything in front of me. All the lights were green; there wasn't a

single break in the circuit that protected the perimeter, which made

some sense considering the alarm wasn't blaring, but confounded me

nevertheless. How had he gotten in, by parachute? At that

moment, I was prepared to believe the most ridiculous reason (except

for the truth, which was *more* than ridiculous). I could see in my

mind's eye all the faces of those who first laughed at me and then

barred me from their oh-so-important societies: one of them must

have decided that I wasn't so crazy after all and went through a lot

of trouble to infiltrate the compound and spy on me, to take my

discoveries away from me and proclaim them his own. He was

waiting outside at that very moment, knowing that he'd been

spotted, and feverishly deciding that the only option was to keep

going, to infiltrate the house and get me out of the way in order to

steal what was mine.

Feeling the cold comfort of the gun in my hand for the first

time, I realized that I hoped he was armed.

It would make what I was going to do to him easier.

Rather than spring out of the house into his waiting rifle-muzzle, I rushed back upstairs until I reached the fourth floor, where the observation point was. It was a cylinder at the top of the stairs with a six-foot radius hatch at its top that had allowed my father and I to gaze at the stars during better days, when science fiction was still just impossible tales to me. When I reached the hatch, I slowly and quietly opened it and peered out through the top, but I never thought of looking at the stars. Though blanketed in fog, I still had a 360-degree view of the grounds below, and I struggled to see any sign of movement. I didn't have long to wait.

Movement... something trudging towards the woods at the back of the compound... apparently dragging something.

With no hope of hitting anything but a tree, I fired through the fog.

An echo-filled "Shit" followed the gunshot. I fired again and heard nothing. I knew he was still out there; he would have made a noise if I'd hit him. I could only assume that he'd made it to the trees, the damned *TREES!* I swore to myself that once this was over that I would have every one of them cut down and turned into the paper that my discoveries would be printed on. I had no choice but to wait there, trying to pierce through the fog for any more movement.

Nearly an hour went by, by which time the Gods smiled on me (at least that's what I thought at the time): the fog was thinning.

I ducked down, with just my eyes and the top of my head sticking above the rim, and I waited.

I saw him at the edge of the woods, skirting from tree to tree, almost as if he knew I was lurking above, waiting for him. Who are you, I thought: Kaminsky... Lennon... Webb?

Yes, Webb... that suck-up toady who wouldn't go away until the ground-breaking theories started coming... then he aligned himself with the establishment... but his face... dying to know what I knew... the look on his face...

Breathing through my teeth, I fired.

His scream was honey on my tongue.

I could've taken him out then and there as he limped into the open and headed for the front gate, could've blown his thick head right off his shoulders. But I held myself back: I wanted to see his face.

I ran downstairs, stepped into loafers, and cautiously stepped out the front door.

"Webb!" I called.

Nothing happened. I spun around, peering in the dark.

"I have a gun, Webb! I'll use it! Don't think that I won't! Come out while you can!"

I waited again. This time, there was rustling off to my right, close to the main gate, in the bushes.

"I see you, Webb! Come out!"

"Don't shoot," he said. "I'm…"

"I'll shoot into the bushes!"

Webb sprang up, his voice choked with pain and sobs. "No, you mustn't…"

I couldn't stop myself: after the gunshot all I could see was the blood and brains exploding out of the back of his head. The only other thing I noticed was the notebook that had flown from his hand landing a few feet behind him.

As I said, I didn't see his face until I went to him; the yard lights were dim but they gave off enough light for me to recognize him. The first thing I noticed was the cut on the right side of his face as if some thin blade had sliced…

That's when I brought a hand up to my own face, on the right side, and felt the clotted blood from the slice I'd gotten from the shattered windowpane.

I looked closer: he was wearing the same clothes that I had hurriedly thrown on an hour before. And his face... once I got past his decimated forehead...

... was *my* face.

The dead man lying before me wasn't Webb: it was me.

I dropped the gun, backed away and ran for the front door, almost stopping short when I saw it was closed. I knew it was open when I ran out to confront Webb (*no not Webb... ME*) and it was standing closed in front of me. I crept up and tried the door; it was locked from the inside. A funny feeling came over me, a truth that needed to be acknowledged in spite of every warning signal in my mind screaming and wailing. Something was happening and, although I didn't want to, I knew I had to get to the ladder that the intruder had placed against the third floor window.

As I ran around the house, I looked up and saw through the heavy fog a bright light shining through the third floor windows where I knew the device was located. Someone has gotten in and is using the device, I frantically thought, trying to push away the other thought that throbbed at the back of my head and demanded to be listened to. I refused to hear it! I knew I *mustn't* hear it! These were the thoughts going through my mind as I ascended the ladder and peeped through the unbroken window of my own master bedroom.

A man was standing there, naked, just having shed the protective suit, and looking at the clock on the wall reading 11:16.

The man was me.

My mouth dropped open.

The fog (*when had it gotten heavy again?*) passed in front of my eyes and I couldn't see myself again until I saw me rearing back to throw the ashtray. I ducked just as the ashtray smashed the glass and I started making my way down the ladder. I stumbled at the last few rungs and fell to the ground, but was up immediately again and running away from my own house.

And yes, I did mutter "Jesus" twice.

Once I'd reached the side of the mansion and was certain that the fog was hiding me (and that I was also currently in the foyer looking at the security map), I took a moment to look at my watch.

It read 10:20.

I'd succeeded... in a way.

I don't know why, but I took it into my head to bury my dead body. You'll never understand what it's like to drag your own dead body into a wood for a shallow burial (Actually, I take that back: you *do* know). I made sure to gather up the notebook that I was holding when I, engulfed in madness, had put a bullet in my brain. I dragged the body the entire length of the mansion and was nearly at the trees when I heard a gunshot and a nearby tree took the bullet that was meant for me. I fell backwards and hurriedly dragged the body the rest of the way into the safety of the woods. There was another shot... and then silence.

I dug with my hands; I deserved better, but the night and fear made me do something I'd never done before: cut corners. With my father's pistol lying on his (*my*) chest, I shoved dirt back into the hole and felt disgusted when I could still see signs of the body lying just below the thin surface of soil.

And there I was, alone in the woods just off my own home, sitting just feet away from my own buried body, with a notebook in my hand.

That's when I read the words that I'd written, words that some earlier version of myself (maybe a million selves ago, for all I know) wrote to warn the next me, the words that you are reading right now. Yes, *You*, the next me, the future me, the paranoid me who believes that Webb is crawling around the compound trying to find a way to steal your secrets away from you. These are the words that will tell you that something went wrong with the device: yes, it *did* succeed, but only partially. Instead of sending you back in time, it created another you (ME! Do you understand what I'm saying?) from an hour before. Somehow that earlier version of you found yourself on the grounds killing an even earlier version of you and then learning the truth. And it has been repeating and repeating ever since. Time is somehow stuck, like a needle on a broken record. You have to fix this somehow before time repeats again! The solution is in the notes; I'm sure of it! Some string of binary numbers got muddled: some zero should be a one! I don't know if it's just me or if the entire universe is stuck in the same timeloop, unknowingly going through the same hour over and over again, but *you* are the one that has to break it. You with the gun and rage on your mind, you must resist the forces of time! If you can't, then maybe I have to...

Shit! I just looked over to where the body was buried so that I could get the gun back, but the mound is gone. Time seems to be

resetting itself! The dirt has never been dug up: the body and the
gun are gone!

My only other option is to sneak in and make the changes
myself. I'm at the edge of the woods and can see the ladder against
the wall twenty yards in front of me. I have to be careful: the fog is
beginning to thin.

You shot me! I shot me! I should've known I couldn't have
made it (none of the earlier versions of me did), but I felt compelled
to try. Now I'm behind the bushes near the front gate. My leg is on
fire and I can barely move. My only hope is to try to make you see
me as I am: I am you! You have to look and keep yourself from
firing. It is the only way to break the timeloop!

I hear the door opening.

You've run to the main gate and you've just shouted "Webb!"

That's me. I know my own voice... I can recognize myself!
You're approaching the bushes. I can see the gun.

Here goes nothing.

Caught Amongst The Banister

(2010)
Marybeth Dresden

I still have the key that Helen gave me; I used it only a couple of times. Maybe I should have just left it on the kitchen table or tossed it into the gutter after I found her on the stairs, but I didn't. It still hangs on my keychain, dull and useless. I'm sure it must be useless after all these years: the house still stands but new people live there now so there's no chance that the locks are still the same.

I wonder what they hear as they walk up and down the stairs, particularly at night.

Helen insisted that I take the key just in case she needed help and couldn't get to the door. But that's not exactly what she said…

In case it won't let me near the door.

I could see that she was scared, but there was never any question that she would come to any harm. That's just Helen, I thought. I mean, don't get me wrong; of course I was worried. How couldn't I have been? But the type of things that she claimed were happening to her, I knew that there was no possible way that any of it could be true.

I *knew* it, you see? I'm practical like that.

If she had been a more energetic type, Helen could have turned her over-active imagination into a fantastic career as a fantasy writer – King and Rowling rolled into one – but instead she lived inside the

shadows of her own making. Too many times during the months that I
knew her, my phone rang at the most absurd hours. I never knew why I
bothered to answer when I knew whose voice I would hear.

Maybe I was, to a certain extent, excited by what she had to say.

"Marybeth, I know that you're going to think that this is stupid,
but I can't deny it anymore: there's someone in this house!"

Or in the garden… or the frog pond… or perched in the old Oak
tree that hung over the roof…

"Strange things are happening," she would say. "You haven't
seen them, but I have!"

"Where?" I would ask.

"In the shadows!"

That's where it always happened… in the shadows. She would
see something move inside the shadows of her home, a home that was
too big for her on her own but which she cherished despite seeing
phantoms and ghoulies jumping about in the darkness. When we first
met at the Spiritualist Society of Somerville, she was a breath of pure,
fine air to our admittedly stodgy bunch. At her first meeting, she
practically glided in on shoes that seemingly didn't quite touch the floor,
all full of questions about the spirit world and her hopes (or expectations)
on what would come to her after death.

"So, how many spirits speak to you during an average sitting?"
she breathlessly asked me the first time she got me alone.

I flushed slightly. "It doesn't really happen like it does in the
movies. Mrs. Lindfors doesn't just open her mouth and voices come
spilling out." Bedelia Lindfors was our regular medium, a prim and

humorless woman who kept herself hidden until we were all seated at the table and never joined us for coffee and cake afterwards. "It's more of a feeling we get: when the moment is right, something... descends upon the table."

"Oh, I see," she said, looking a trifle crestfallen.

"I'm afraid if you're looking for a windstorm or a shaking table, you might be disappointed." We had had several like her before, daffy dingbats with money who gave no thought to the spirit world other than as an alternative to seeing a revival of *Mama Mia* at the Wang. Most of them were polite, smiled after the session, thanked us from the bottom of their hearts and rarely turned up a second time. I decided to press her. "What exactly are you looking for from our society?"

Helen sipped her tea (no alcohol was allowed until after the session was finished) and looked uneasy. "I don't think I know yet."

The session consisted of nine of us, including Mrs. Lindfors, situated at the table. Helen sat next to me and held my hand gently. I could feel the excitement throbbing just underneath her thumb, but she was otherwise still and silent. That was unusual; most new guests had to be chided by Mrs. Lindfors to remain quiet or risk disturbing the "ether." I found myself wondering if the drone of Mrs. Lindfors's voice was instead lulling Helen to sleep. I endeavored to peek.

"Concentrate so that we can open the path through which those who have passed before us may travel... let the curtain slide gently aside... let... Marybeth, *CONCENTRATE!*"

She always seemed to know who was not trying hard enough and felt no need to keep quiet about it. I felt Doris momentarily grip my other hand tighter in a silent reproach. From Helen I felt nothing, her grip did not tighten nor relax.

It was another twelve minutes before Mrs. Lindfors's voice faded and that strange familiar feeling began to come over me. My head dropped backwards slightly and it felt like maybe unseen fingers had gently grasped my temples, guiding and supporting me. I wanted to breathe deeper because the air tasted different, like it sparkled with electricity, but I remembered the time when Jenny Coffey hyperventilated and passed out at the table so I kept my breathing slow and even. The only thing I was truly conscious of as that heavenly wave rolled over me was my hands, each one grasped by my neighbors, anchoring me to the world I belonged in. What was hovering above me (if anything, if I may allow my natural skepticism to break the mood for a moment) I didn't know; maybe it was nothing more than the incense and Mrs. Lindfors's voice lulling me into a state of naïve acceptance. Sometimes I thought I could catch a faint whiff of my great-aunt Vera's own special scent, a mixture of sweet perfume, face powder and a waft of Beefeaters. Mrs. Lindfors never dissuaded me from my belief – she always said that a visitation could take any form and affect any sense – and I did little to talk myself out of it. I don't really believe that Great Aunt Vera was visiting me at those sessions, and yet I do.

The spell was presently broken, not abruptly but broken nevertheless, and I found myself sitting as usual in my seat with my neighbors' hands in mine. I sniffed and felt my eyes holding back a tear or two, again as usual. My great-aunt Vera always did that to me: so delicate and cherished was her memory (I chose to ignore the fact that it was cirrhosis that did her in just two weeks shy of my seventh birthday) that I always wished she'd greet me with one of her infectious and raucous laughs rather than just her scent. A finer woman than my great-aunt Vera never lived.

I looked around and saw that the other ladies were experiencing very similar aftereffects: some had light tears on their cheeks, others were fanning themselves and none of them were frowning. Well...

Helen wasn't exactly *frowning*, but she wasn't exactly smiling either. She was sitting there on my right, still holding my hand and staring in a slightly dazed manner at the opposite wall. She was not entranced; I could see her jaw working as if she was trying to solve a particularly tricky trig problem. She didn't react to my letting her hand loose or to any of the soft chatter around her.

"Helen?" I wasn't sure if I should disturb her, so I spoke softly. The others at the table heard me anyway and, being as they were interested in what the new girl thought, they put their own personal revelations on hold. Helen turned to me, keeping her eyes fixed on that same spot on the wall a moment longer before giving me her full attention.

"Yes?"

"That's it, I'm afraid," I said.

She stole another quick look at the wall. I looked too; it was nothing but a shadow cast by the hope chest.

"Okay," she said.

With that, the other ladies at the table got up and began making their way to the coffee and cookies that had been laid out earlier, all except the two women on either side of Mrs. Lindfors, whose duty it was to help the apparently exhausted woman to her feet and lead her to whatever backroom she preferred, keeping herself away from prying eyes and questions from those who wanted interpretations as to what they had experienced. After a half an hour or so, she would leave by the back way and the society would partake of the wine and spirits in the cabinet.

After Mrs. Lindfors started for her sanctuary, the table was empty except for the two of us. Helen was looking at me with a weak smile, but something in her face told me that something else was on her mind.

"Would you like some coffee?" I asked.

She ignored my question and asked her own. "So you do this only once a week?"

* * *

So Helen became one of us. She came faithfully, got to know the other ladies and proved to have a marvelous knowledge of theater, botany, wine and basketball (not many of the other members cared much for that, but she never stopped trying to turn them all into Celtics fans). The other women liked her at first. I never stopped liking her, despite everything that happened later.

The fifth session was when I first noticed it.

The session was over and there was nothing strange or even worth noting. I was letting my fond memories of dear Vera fade away and was just about to partake of a particularly delectable-looking donut when Helen's nails caught me in the arm and I nearly dropped my coffee. "Ow! Helen, what the Hell is…"

"There!"

She pointed to the wall. There wasn't much to see: an area between the couch and the end table, close to the floor and darkened in shadow.

"What?" I was hoping she was not going to say the word "mouse" and send the room into an uproar.

"I saw something move."

"A bug or something?"

She didn't answer right away but she shook her head. No one but me noticed any of this.

"It... looked at me."

I laughed; I couldn't help it. "It *looked* at you?"

"Uh..."

"What did it look like?"

She looked away for a moment and didn't turn back to answer. "Upset."

* * *

During the next three sessions, I noticed a change in Helen's grip.

I also noticed a change in the attitude of some of the other members: Helen had apparently whispered a thing or two to someone else and it had gotten around. I could tell from the looks that she was getting that the prevailing opinion about her was changing.

Odd, don't you think?

She kept staring at a shadow...

I'm not sure I feel comfortable...

The session after that was held at her house.

The society didn't have a set meeting place; we all took turns hosting Mrs. Lindfors. Once Helen had been with us for a time, it was only natural that she would want to sponsor the society at her own home. And what a home it was: not a mansion but not the squat front-to-backs that we were used to. It stood not entirely alone: there were other houses on her street, but none of them were as far down the dead-end road as hers and the trees didn't seem to engulf the others quite as much. It stood sturdy and defiant against the foliage that seemed intent on crowding it away from the road. It stood strong and white and stuck out amongst the dusk as we arrived.

There was something about it that I didn't like.

Helen greeted us warmly and directed us to the kitchen where the platter of pastries was laid out. The room smelled richly of coffee and the women were entranced by the scope of the house and the beautiful country-style decorations that adorned the walls. The ladies tucked into the refreshments like hungry ghouls and chatted about how marvelous it was to have a new venue in which to pierce the veil. Helen flitted about, excited and, to my eyes anyway, seemingly close to hysteria. I was able to pull her aside once the last guest arrived and handed her a coffee.

"So, Mrs. Lindfors is here, I take it," I said.

"In a spare room upstairs. She wouldn't take a thing I offered her when she first arrived, not even a glass of water. She started sniffing around the living room, all around the table and along the walls. Good thing I dusted before she got here or…"

"She does that," I said, seeing that Helen was starting to get herself worked up again. "Tell me, has this house been in your family?"

"Oh no, and I know what you're thinking: it's too big for just little me. Yes, I know that. But it reminds me of the house my family lived in when I was a little girl in West Bridgewater. Did you grow up in a big house? No? Oh, it's magic! The hours of fun that my brother and I had running through the halls and hiding from each other in the millions of nooks just came flooding back to me when I first saw this house. I know how silly that sounds: I won't be running and hiding in here now that most of my family is gone, but my husband left me well off and..."

"...I didn't know you were married," I said, "I'm sorry."

Helen blinked and she cleared her throat. "No matter. I'm used to it by now." She gave me a look that told me she wasn't used to it in any way. "But I do love walking into this house, seeing it open before me..."

There was a loud series of knocks on the ceiling. All the women immediately stopped chattering and looked up.

"Oh, she must be ready," said Helen. "She said she would do that. Everyone please go into the next room; there's a table that should just fit us all and I'll go and get Mrs. Lindfors."

The table in the next room was a bit smaller than what we would've been comfortable with - I felt slightly squeezed in my place - but there was enough room and we all settled into our places as Helen led Mrs. Lindfors down the stairs. Halfway down, Mrs. Lindfors seemed unsure of her footing, but her firm hold of Helen's hand kept her going and she came over to the table and sat down without a word. Helen sat next to her.

We all joined hands.

I closed my eyes, leaned my head back and waited.

"And now we place ourselves in the hands of the spirits to guide us through to the next land… where bodies are vapors… where thoughts are mists… where dreams are the roadways that connect their land to ours. We call upon those lonely spirits to grace us with their gifts… to show us… *NOOOO! CHRIST, NOOOOOOOOO!"*

We all jumped in our places as Mrs. Lindfors howled in horror, her eyes fixed on the ceiling. We all let go of each others' hands, but Mrs. Lindfors refused to relinquish her grip on the hands of her neighbors, one of whom was Helen.

"She's breaking my fingers!"

"STOP IT! GO AWAY! STAY AWAY FROM ME!"

Some of the women were so shocked that they couldn't move. I covered my ears to block out the screams. I wanted to turn away, but I was compelled to watch Mrs. Lindfors, rigid and terror-stricken, staring up at the ceiling while Helen and Janis – the woman on Mrs. Lindfors's right – tried to release their hands from her grip. Another one of the women, Molly Carlisle, finally found the presence of mind to jump up and try to help. She reached Mrs. Lindfors just as Helen finally pulled her hand free and Janis let out a scream.

"Jesus, my hand!"

Mrs. Lindfors was still screaming and, having no one to hold on to, she tried to claw at Helen's shoulder, but the frightened woman jumped out of her way. Molly got her arms around Mrs. Lindfors, but she seemed to take no notice. The screaming continued.

"NO! NO! NO! WHATEVER YOU ARE, GET OUT OF HERE! AAAGGGGGHHHH!"

Most of the women had, by now, leapt up from the table and huddled against the wall, only Molly, Helen, Janis and myself remained with the writhing woman. Finally, when Molly realized that holding her was doing no good, she wrapped her arm in front of the terrified woman's eyes. Mrs. Lindfors didn't fight her; she slowly stopped flailing in her chair and the screams died into a raspy trickle of air from her mouth. I moved closer and heard Molly whispering to her.

"There's nothing there, Bedelia... nothing... calm down... whatever it is... it's over... it's gone... just like you told it to... now I'm gonna take my arm away... calm down... it's alright... just let me take my arm away and show you... there's nothing there..."

Molly slowly uncovered Mrs. Lindfors's eyes. The woman tentatively opened them and looked to the ceiling. The entire room held its breath.

Her eyes darted around, but she was silent. Molly gently released her. Mrs. Lindfors wiped away her tears and looked all around the room to make sure. Evidently, nothing was there.

Molly leaned close and gently said, "What was it?"

Mrs. Lindfors's only response was a cold look in Helen's direction before she sprang up from her chair and ran for the stairs. One of us should have cautioned her, shouted out for her to be careful, but we were too shocked. Only the sound of Mrs. Lindfors yelling and the thuds as she tumbled down the stairs brought us back.

She was lying at the foot of the stairs when we reached her, moaning. A bulge in her shoulder told me that it was probably dislocated.

"Nobody touch her," I yelled.

"I'll call an ambulance," I heard Helen say, but I didn't pay much attention to her. I leaned closer to Mrs. Lindfors.

"Don't try to move, Bedelia. There's a doctor coming. What happened; did you slip?"

She tried to shake her head, but the pain was too great. Instead, she breathed:

"It was waiting for me... on the stairs."

* * *

There weren't any more meetings for the next three weeks; Mrs. Lindfors's shoulder healed up much faster than her memories of that night (whatever they were – she never told us what she saw). When we finally saw her again, she looked old and frightened and it took three more sessions before she could bring herself to successfully call the spirits back again. There was no talk about ever holding another session at Helen's house. There was no need to; Helen never came to the sessions again, a move that I found understandable but upsetting nevertheless. I couldn't see any reason why Helen should have blamed herself for what happened... yes, I admit that there was something about her house that I didn't like at first, but Helen had been as sweet and as generous as any of the rest of us on our hosting nights and I wanted to reassure her that Mrs. Lindfors's strange turn couldn't have possibly been her fault.

I kept in touch with her, calling her every few days to make sure she was alright. At first she sounded distant on the phone, not interested in anything I had to say but making sure to sound grateful enough for my attention.

After three or four calls, her tone began to change.

"Marybeth, I had this really strange dream the other night..."

I was too quick to reassure her. "We've all been having some strange nights since..."

"No, no; this has been happening long before that night. I didn't want to talk about it at first because I really didn't know you all that well. I've been having a version of this dream, on and off, ever since my husband died. I... Marybeth... I can only imagine what you must think of me."

I was caught completely off guard by that; I hadn't known Helen very long but had begun to like her very much. She'd struck me as someone who was searching for something, but didn't want anyone else to know about it for fear that she'd be ridiculed. There was definitely no vindictiveness in her nature or the vacant "impress-me" boredom of the average housewife. I'd suspected that the Helen I'd first met was someone trying to escape a great gray creature that had been stalking her ever since she'd been widowed: a beast called "isolation."

"Did I ever tell you how my husband died?"

"Helen, I didn't even know you were married until that last session."

She spoke over me. "I found him at the bottom of the stairs. I think he might have been there for hours. I came in the front door, all ready to show him what I'd bought… I had a great jacket that I knew would fit him perfectly. All I wanted was to see his face sitting on top of that stupid jacket, smiling at me. Everything on him was twisted: his neck, his arms, his legs, his ankles…"

She fell into silence after that and I wished that she'd been sitting next to me so that I could hug her, but all I had was the slight heaving of her breath on the other end of the phone. I didn't really know what to say that she hadn't heard already. "Helen, I'm so sorry for…"

"That's when I first started seeing the eyes in my sleep. Just eyes in the darkness… looking and looking and searching for me… Marybeth…" and then her voice fell into sobs, "I never thought it would take Jack from me"

Three days later, an envelope came in the mail. Inside was a key wrapped around a handwritten note: I might need you. I think it's hiding nearby. Please be ready.

From there began the regular calls: something was coming and she could see it following her in the car as she came home from the supermarket; it hung precariously balanced from the tallest branch of the willow tree and looked away when she thought she caught site of it. I'll always remember how she described it:

Like a Cheshire cat minus the smile…

That frightened me more than I ever thought it could. I jumped into the car and drove to Helen's house. I used the key to enter without even knocking or using the bell. From the door I could see a pool of light in the front room, where the horrific sitting had taken place. I started going to her.

"Helen?"

"I know it's you," she said, her voice choked. "I can tell by your shoes. I'm in here."

Once I got to the edge of the front room, I beheld a woman that I wasn't sure I'd ever met before: she was sitting alone on the couch that could have sat three with three things on the coffee table in front of her: a glass, an ice bucket, and a bottle of Gordon's gin.

"Helen, what are you doing?"

"I knew it was your shoes," she said, apparently not paying attention to my concern. "You're wearing your blue flats. They make a distinct 'clack' when you walk." She looked up at me standing in the doorway. Her eyes crossed for a moment and I stole a look at the bottle; it was less than half full. "Please don't think I have some sort of weird fetish over what your shoes sound like, although they *are* cute shoes. I've always been able to detect so much from a person's footsteps. Ever since I was child I've always had a thing about footsteps: how heavy they were, how fast, what they were wearing. I had to, you see. My brother used to love to creep up on me when we were kids: he'd tickle me. When I least expected it, I'd feel his fingers grab my sides or he'd start scrabbling at my feet. God, I used to *scream*."

I took the opportunity of her refreshing her glass to sit down next to her. She wasn't very old, not past forty from all I could see, but when she turned to me and lifted the glass to her mouth, she looked as old as Great Aunt Vera did the last time I saw her. The alcohol had relaxed most of her body, all except her toes which were grabbing at the dust ruffle.

"So I got to know his footsteps, Marybeth; his more than anyone's. Father's were heavy and often unsteady, the result of too many kisses with bottles like this. Mom would almost float around the kitchen: if any person on this planet could have achieved the art of flight, it would have been my mother. Peter..." she paused and took another drink, "... Peter knew how to sneak around the house. I got to know it: I could hear him coming a mile away in socks."

She took another drink and nearly choked on it. I reached for the glass but she pulled it away. Instead, she looked into my eyes and I wanted to cry: the woman that I'd met and held an affinity for had turned into a frightened and shivering lush.

"I can hear him here, Marybeth... his stocking feet are padding around this house as we speak! He's keeping his distance because you're here; he doesn't want anyone to see what he's going to do."

She pulled up a second glass that I hadn't seen when I'd first entered. I tried to demur, but when she lapsed into silence, I let her fix me a drink. It felt good from the first sip.

"I got good at playing tricks on him, you know," she said after clinking her glass with mine. "I got him a few times." First she chuckled, as if lost in old dear memories. But when she looked at me, she looked like she was begging me for forgiveness.

"I didn't mean it... I just kicked him... I didn't know any better."

For another hour, she talked about TV shows, daylilies, shoes and Rajon Rondo before she let her delicate head drift into the couch's cushions. I stretched her out on the couch and poured out the rest of the gin before I left, taking one last look at her to make sure she was alright.

I think I would've kissed her forehead if I had known...

* * *

That wasn't the last time I saw her, though I wish it had been.

At Helen's funeral, I met her last living relative, her aunt Mia who wept only sparingly and smelt of Beefeaters, but differently from Aunt Vera. In a place called the Memorial Café, I took the time to tweeze out a few facts concerning her little brother Peter.

"They were lovely children, both of them. A couple of scamps, they'd chase each other and roll around all day. It was so tragic how Peter came to his end. It was Helen who found him: there she was at the bottom of the stairs, crying her poor little eyes out with Peter up there, caught amongst the banister. He'd tried to stick his head between the railings like so many children do and apparently got it stuck. Most of them just stay there until they cry for help and someone comes running. But Peter somehow managed to lose his footing on the stairs: we found him with his legs splayed down the steps and his head still jammed in the railings, his eyes staring out in horror. I wish I knew how he'd managed to break his neck like that. I don't know what was more horrifying: little Peter's cold dead stare or Helen's crying and moaning at her little brother's body."

The only reason why she didn't know what was more horrifying was because Helen's casket had been closed at her funeral. There was no other choice.

The mortician had seen what I'd seen that last time after I'd failed to get Helen on the phone and rushed over to her house. I'd run in, panicked and not wanting to believe anything could have been true about the drunken rant she'd given me only a week before. I'd prayed so hard as I ran across her kitchen floor, hoping Helen would call out and tell me that she recognized my shoes again.

But then I found her.

Eyes in the darkness… looking for me… I didn't mean it… I just kicked him…

When I think of it now, all I can hear is the howl of a little girl who'd innocently kicked the legs out from under her little brother, not even thinking about the possibility that the poor little child, caught amongst the banister, would strangle as a result.

And all I can see are her eyes, staring at the wall, from the head that had been horribly squeezed and mutilated after something had forced it through the railings of the banister.

Look At Me!

(1993)
C.J. McCarthy

Look at me, he thought, willing the girl sitting at the bar with her friends to get her nose out of her Manhattan and turn her head towards him. He'd blocked out all the noise around him, particularly whatever nonsense Denise was prattling on about; in the entire club, despite a good crowd for a Friday, there was only himself and the girl at the bar with the long chestnut hair, tight yellow tank top and gold ballet flats that dangled from her toes. He concentrated harder and thought he saw the girl laugh more distractedly at one of her friends' jokes, as if some force was pulling her attention elsewhere. He imagined that she thought that there might be a fly in the vicinity, buzzing around her ears, but that impression wouldn't last long.

*Soon now, just a bit more concentration… just arch my eyebrows… just a bit… Denise won't notice… stupid cunt… look at me, darling… there's no other man here but me… me and my saus*eeege*… you'll see me and you won't believe your…*

She turned her head, just like he knew she would, and caught a good long glance at him. Like always, he was sure to turn his attention back to Denise so that the girl at the bar caught his strong profile and didn't get a hint that he might, in any way, be interested in her. Maybe he'd take Denise home after this last drink and come back for her or maybe he wouldn't. It really didn't matter; he gotten her attention without letting on to Denise and that was a win in his book.

"Eduardo?"

His complexion didn't hint at Spanish blood for the simple reason that he didn't have any, but "Eduardo" sounded better than "Eddie" and all the girls seemed to believe him when he said he was named after a distant Spanish relative. "Yeah?" he asked, sounding only slightly bored.

"Are you alright? Did something happen at work?"

He shook his head and sighed. "Just tired after a long week; you know how it is. Maybe went a few minutes too long at the gym."

Denise's response was immediate. "You didn't hurt yourself, did you? You shouldn't work out so hard; you're in perfect shape and you probably don't need to exert yourself so much. Besides, I'd like a bit of flab on you."

Lyin' hole. I know what you want in a man and this is it... you want me to look this way forever and I just might, but not for you... if you could only hear with my ears for just a minute while you're talking... can you actually be anything but bored stupid at all the dumbass shit you talk... I can just barely remember when I found you interesting... so long ago... three weeks and before you opened your mouth... thank Christ I'm not going to have to listen to your shit much lon...

Something just short of a sharp pain flirted with the left side of his neck and his head jerked to the side. He grunted and his knee knocked the underside of the table, shuddering the drinks but not hard enough to upend them.

"Eduardo," Denise said in mid-gasp, "what is it? You okay?"

His hand was already pressed against his neck as he gritted his teeth and waited for the pain to subside. "Yeah, yeah, might be a muscle spasm, I guess," he said, knowing it wasn't. It had been a strange glancing flair against his skin and he could feel a few drops of blood on his fingertips, although he'd say nothing of the sort to Denise because her concern was even more boring than her usual fawning attention.

Before giving Denise an arched eyebrow and smile to show that he was okay and thinking about getting her panties off, he stole a quick look around the room again and was pleased to find the girl of chestnut hair and gold flats still looking at him.

Later...

He cracked his neck, flashed an "I'm-completely-fine" smile to Denise and brought out his wallet to pay for the drinks.

$12.75... a bargain.

Two hours later, spent but still looking perfect, he returned to the bar and wasn't surprised to see that the girl whose eye he'd caught had gone home. Instead, he chatted with a girl with black hair named Dorothy and no longer felt spent.

Certainly Dorothy didn't think so.

And neither the spasm nor the scratch on his neck entered his mind the entire night.

* * *

When he woke up the next morning, past ten o'clock (but that was okay because it was Saturday and he'd needed the sleep), he strolled into the kitchen and nearly blurted out a horselaugh when he saw what was written on the whiteboard attached to the refrigerator, the one with the heading THINGS TO DO: *call Dorothy 612-322-4788!*

Yeah, right, he thought, that's something I must do right away. Ooooh, ooooh, I wonder if I should call her now and risk waking her up since I can't stand to not hear her voice for another minute. I hope I remembered to charge my phone last night or I'll just go nuts!

He chuckled as he erased Dorothy's helpful hint from his whiteboard and scribbled in a few things he knew he needed to pick up from the market. He mused on how a simple wipe of the cloth (and his strict rule that no girls were allowed to sleep over after sex, a rule he enforced with a lie concerning a promise he'd made to an imaginary, puritanical landlord) effectively erased Dorothy from his life, with the exception of her scent on his sheets and the sticky and wrinkled rubber in the trash. And, of course, his memory of her, which was strong and life-affirming, although he knew it would fade in a matter of days so that even her name would be forgotten by this time next week. He might see her again, at the bar or along the street; she might even come into the showroom some day to get a new car, but her pretty face would stir only the barest of responses from him and her name would completely escape him. She'd get the message and move on. What did you expect from a guy that picked you up in a bar past midnight anyway, a ring and a book on effective parenting?

"You got exactly what you knew you'd get," he said, not sure why he was muttering to an empty room, "so stop with the 'call me' jazz. If I want you, I'll let you know."

The phone rang and he let the machine get it. Denise wanted to know if he wanted to go to the park that day and have a picnic by the lake. Do they serve martinis there, he thought before deciding that it was time that the outgoing message on his machine was going to be the only thing that Denise heard from him from now on. And if she put up a fuss, well... that was nothing new. He had friends at work he could hook her up with and take her off his hands. He'd done it before.

Eddie pulled a kiwi fruit out of a bowl on the counter, sectioned it, and slowly ate it, wondering why he'd never tasted a woman as good. He felt vital again as he swallowed the pulp and only briefly appeared out of sorts at his reflection in the kitchen window when the scab on his neck came into view. What with all the activity from the night before, he'd forgotten feeling the sting while sitting in the bar and naturally assumed that either Denise or Dorothy had bitten him in a moment of passionate abandon.

Oh well, he thought, at least it's not a hickey.

* * *

Look at me...

The girl from the night before, formally of the tank top and ballet flats but now in jeans and tee-shirt and filling out a Keno card on the other side of the bar, looked up. He was careful to lower his eyes and make it look natural by taking another sip of his drink. It was early, only four in the afternoon, and he had come in straight from the gym simply to relax, check out the ball scores and see if anyone even remotely interesting would wander in. He certainly wasn't expecting to see the girl from the night before, but there she was, looking more casual but still ripe and ready for plucking, her pert breasts swelling against the lime-green shirt and begging to be freed.

The lady bartender, young and pretty with ginger hair, saw that his drink was nearly finished and made her way over. "You need another?"

"Sure," he said, "a bit less vermouth this time… uh…"

"Jamyn," she said. She'd only been working there a few weeks and he didn't know her as well as the other bartenders.

"Jamyn, right. You've told me that before, right?"

"Yeah, but lots of people have trouble with it at first."

"Yeah, I guess you don't hear it every day, do you?"

"Well," she said, smiling at him, "*I* hear it every day."

Eddie chuckled, a bit embarrassed. "Oh yeah, well, you would, wouldn't you? It's your name, isn't it?"

"We've established that already." She had already turned away to start fixing his martini and he was grateful for the opportunity to shut his mouth. There was something about lady bartenders that were not only immune to his natural charms but also turned his usual gift for chat into a stumbling mess. He guessed it was because they'd seen guys like him before by the dozen, sidling up to bars and trying to be smooth with whatever pair of tits that crossed into their line of sight. This girl, like all the others who tended bars, had gotten a God's-eye view of his action and could spot it coming from a mile away. Never once, in his entire life, had he ever asked a bartender of the fairer sex what she was gonna do after her shift was over.

Besides, if he ever wanted to get a drink in this place again, he knew enough to leave the staff alone.

Being so preoccupied with his thoughts, he nearly missed the girl from the night before suddenly look into her own drink to hide the fact that she was looking at him.

Conquest, he thought without betraying it on his face. Jamyn put his fresh martini in front of him.

"Wanna know her name?" she asked.

"No thanks, I'll find out soon enough." He looked at her, wondering if she would object to his cockiness. She merely shrugged.

"Just thought I'd save you the trouble."

"It's no trouble." He thought he could see her stiffen slightly as she turned away and he smiled into his drink.

Yeah, I thought so… don't like it when a guy like me comes in and does what comes natural when it comes to the ladies, do you? Sisterhood and all that crap. Can't do anything about it, can you, because I'm just sitting here, minding my own business and not bothering anybod...

"Hi," a pretty voice said on his right. She'd startled him, but he didn't show it; only his brown eyes (which he'd often been told were his best feature) darted suddenly in her direction. She'd made what she'd thought was the first move, not realizing that he'd been reeling her in, gently but firmly, for nearly the last twenty hours. Best to let the catch think it's made up it's own mind to wind up in the net. Why put up with that kind of a struggle.

"My name's Eduardo," he said. "But I answer to 'Eddie', if you like."

"I like Eduardo…"

Gotcha!

"…you don't hear it very often."

Eddie smiled. "Well… I hear it every day."

Thanks Jamie, or whatever the Hell your name is.

The girl laughed. "That's funny. I'm Kitty."

Kitty with the titties, he didn't say. "Pleased to meet you." Instead of shaking her hand, he lifted his drink as if toasting her. She did the same and finished off the last swallow of her white wine. "Would you like another?"

"I saw you here last night, I think. Was that you?"

She's pretending to be unsure in order to sound nonchalant. She knows it was me.

"You were sitting at a table over there… with a girl."

"Yeah, Denise." He was much better at sounding nonchalant than she was. "So, who were you here with last night?"

"Oh… just a friend."

He used his best features to look deeper into her. "Me too."

He was about to savor the look of relief that he knew was going to cross her face when something sharp tore against his left side, a few inches below his armpit. He gasped and couldn't bite back a good, hearty "Shit!"

"What? What happened?" She put a hand on his shoulder, not knowing what else to do.

"I… goddammit, what the Hell was that?" He peeled open his collar to peer down his shirt.

"Are you hurt?"

No, Dummy, I always jerk and shout when I meet a pretty girl... it's part of the fertility rites of my people...

Lifting up his arm, he could just make out a splash of red running down his ribs.

"I'm bleeding!"

"What?"

He ignored her and looked towards Jamyn, who was obliviously chewing gum and staring at the Keno numbers. "Jamie, have you got rats in here or something?"

"What?" She hadn't noticed anything.

"Something... bit me!"

She stopped chewing long enough to make a face. "What?"

"Are you being dense just for fun? I said, I've been bitten!"

"Where?"

"On my side!"

Jamyn came closer and Kitty got off her stool and went to his other side to see the wound. Both women peered over as he lifted his arm, reflecting on how this probably wasn't his sexiest pose.

"Jesus, you're bleeding," said Kitty.

"Yeah, I know that!" he said, completely out of patience.

"Okay, sorry."

"Just tell me what it looks like."

Jamyn spoke up next. "You're gonna have to lift up your shirt."

"What?"

"There's blood on your shirt, but it's not torn. Just lift it up."

His hands started shaking as he lifted up his shirt. "You guys are really screwed, you know that? I'm gonna have the health department down here. I don't know what you've got scuttling around down here but…"

"Oh my God!" Kitty said no more as she'd clasped her hand over her mouth.

"How big is it?" Neither of them answered and his hands shook even more. "How big do rats get anyw…"

Jamyn cut him off. "It wasn't a rat."

Eddie felt his skull about to blow apart. "Well, it wasn't a fucking tiger, was it?"

The two women ignored him and muttered to each other.

"Why didn't it touch his shirt?"

"Was there anybody else creeping around… like… hiding out of my sight just beneath the bar?"

"WHAT THE FUCK ARE YOU TWO TALKING ABOUT?"

"Somebody bit you."

He looked up at Kitty, who had gone pale white. "Somebody…"

"It looks human, Eduardo. It's just the size of a mouth and the teeth marks are…"

"Don't be so fucking stupid!"

"Don't talk that way to me!" she shouted. "I'm trying to help!"

There had only been three or four other customers in the bar, but they had all wandered over by this time to see what the commotion was. Eddie felt sickened by all the eyes that were training themselves on him as he sat, shaking and with his shirt hoisted up to his armpits. He could feel the blood tickling as it traced down his side and started collecting at his waist. The voices weren't loud, but they were attacking his ears just the same.

"Christ, what is that?"

"Did he come in here with that?"

"That ain't right!"

The sweat dripping into his eyes, plus Jamyn shouting for everyone to go back to their drinks and give him some room, woke him up again. He slowly began to lower his shirt and found himself unsteadily getting to his feet.

"You want me to call an ambulance?"

All he wanted to do was slink home and forget that the last ten minutes had ever happened. "I'll be alright. I just have to…"

The bartender's voice seemed far away. "I can't let you leave like this. Sit down and I'll have a doctor here in a few minutes."

But Eddie didn't listen to anything except the two words repeating in his head as he headed for the door.

Gotta Go… Gotta Go… Gotta Go… Gotta Go… Gotta…

And then something grabbed his ear, pulled it back and tore a part of it away. Eddie screamed and slapped his hand against his head. Then he felt another chunk get ripped out of the small of his back and he fell backwards to the floor.

The sound of running feet accompanied a portion of his bicep being bitten away. He looked up and saw a crowd of dumb-looking faces, as well as Jamyn still chewing her gum, staring down at him as he passed out.

* * *

When he came to in the hospital, almost every inch of his body was tightly wrapped up and throbbing deeper and harder than Zulu war drums. A confused-looking male nurse was standing over him; the second he discerned that Eddie was waking up, he turned and called for a doctor whom Eddie tried to see but found his neck too painful to twist towards. Instead he waited for the doctor to come within his line of vision. For the first time in recent memory, Eddie was unimpressed by the female doctor's obvious comeliness. In fact, he wanted nothing more than to cover himself with a sheet until the attractive woman went away.

"Mr. Bowman," she said gently, "can you hear me?"

He tried to nod.

"I would suggest talking if you can."

Slowly, a voice he barely recognized said, "I'm listening."

She signaled for the nurse to leave them alone before continuing. "This is going to sound like a crazy question, Mr. Bowman, but has anything like this ever happened to you before?"

"N-n-n-n-not before la-sssst night… at the bar… f-f-f-f-felt like a… s-s-sssting."

"In the same bar you were in today?"

"Yesssssssss."

She sat back, nearly out of his line of sight, and he was worried that she would just leave him there, filled with pain and unanswered questions. "D-d-doctor, isss there… sssomething at the bar that… d-d-d-did thisssssss…"

"Mr. Bowman, we have several witnesses from the bar, both staff and patrons, who say that when you fell to the floor, bites just started... appearing on you. Mostly under your clothes, but where the skin was exposed, like on your neck and the tip of your nose, people got a clear view of..."

Eddie, ignoring the pain in his arm, reached up and touched his bandaged nose. The doctor gently took his wrist and tried to coax the arm back down to his side. "Please, Mr. Bowman, you have to give yourself time..."

"My f-f-f-ffface..."

"...doesn't concern me as much as the fact that whatever it was that was biting you went for your jugular vein. If it wasn't for the manager at the bar, who got his hand in there before you lost too much blood, we wouldn't be talking now. As it stands, we've counted a total of twenty-three wounds on you in various places as high as your left eyebrow and as low as the back of your right shin. While most are shallow, at least four are deep enough to have taken some muscle tissue. Plus, your left earlobe and the tip of your nose have been bitten off. Now, no one in the bar can say where the missing flesh is. No one saw the earlobe on the floor, only the blood from the wound. There doesn't seem to be any infection as far as I can see, which is the best possible news I can give you. You've been shot up with antibiotics, stitched and patched up as best as we can. I would suggest you stay here for a while until you get your strength back and heal. Down the road, you may want to consider surgery to correct some of the more lasting damage. But my main concern is what caused this, Mr. Bowman; frankly, I'm stumped."

He breathed a few times, waiting for the dizziness to pass, before trying to speak. "Sssssomething in that... God Damned Bar!"

"Mr. Bowman, you have to calm yourself down; don't make it any worse."

"Look at me! How much worse can it get?"

* * *

He felt ready to go home after thirty-six hours; actually, he wasn't ready to move at all, but the word about the mysterious man-eaten patient had passed through the hospital quicker than a staph infection and head after head poked through the doorway to get a peek at him. Every orderly, nurse and doctor (all of whom were showing a definite lack of professional ethics) who had business anywhere near the vicinity of his ward found themselves dropping in to see for themselves. A screen was placed around him, but he could still see the silhouettes of disappointed would-be gawkers. Eddie imagined that it would only be a matter of time before the hospital installed a carnival barker at the ward entrance shouting "Hurry, hurry, hurry; step right up and see the eighth wonder of the world! You've seen thalidomide babies; you've seen industrial accidents from the turn of the century, but you've never seen the Enigmatic Eduardo, the Amazing Half-Eaten Man! Hunted and tortured by teeth that only he can see and feel, Eduardo sports twenty-three – count them – twenty-three human bite marks on his body. Where will the phantom strike next? Stick around and wait, ladies and gentlemen, because waiting's half the fun!"

It hurt to walk on his bitten leg, but he gathered up enough strength to get out of bed and say that he would sign any release they put in front of him if it meant that he could just get the Hell out of there.

Finally, claiming to be a Christian Scientist and threatening to bring a suit against the hospital for oppressing his religious beliefs did the trick.

He nearly passed out in the cab on the way home and the walk from the street to his front door was excruciating. On his way up to his front door, he met up with the old woman who lived in the apartment above him on the stairs. She was shocked by his appearance and tried to help him the rest of the way, but he swatted her reaching hands away.

"Just get out of here and don't look at me!"

She left him to make his own way.

He slumped into a chair at his kitchen table and, for the first time, started feeling all over his body to see where he had been hurt. He felt the stitches above his eye, wrinkled his nose and felt the missing part sting, and found that there were few muscles he could move that didn't tug at the stitches and bandages holding them together. He gently, over a matter of minutes, took off his shirt and gingerly let his fingers trail down his chest.

There was a jagged scab trailing the curve of his right pectoral. His fingers found stitches curving around his navel. Further down, reaching into his pants, he felt more stitches on the inside of his thigh. And there was no getting away from the pain on the side of his neck or the throbbing in his leg. There was no way of getting away from any of it. It was all real.

What the fuck happened to me? What the...

His breath hitched and, for the first time since he was fourteen, he started crying.

He would've stayed sitting slumped at the table all night, with his head bobbing with tears, if there hadn't been a knock at the door.

His voice was streaked with tears as he shouted "WHO IS IT?"

"It's Jamyn... from the bar."

"GO AWAY!"

"I called the hospital and they said that you'd left."

Well obviously, dumbass...

"Yes," he shouted, although with less energy. "I'm no longer at the hospital. I didn't want people staring at me. I suppose that sounds stupid to you!"

There was a pause and then, awkwardly, "No."

Neither of them said anything for a moment. Eddie counted twelve throbs in his leg before a squeak on the stairs told him that she was still there, waiting for him.

"What do you want?"

He thought that he could hear her gulp before she answered. "Can I come in?"

"NO!"

"Eddie, everyone at the bar is very concerned about you..."

"The doctor said it wasn't rat bites, so you guys are in the clear. There ain't nothing I can sue you for. You can tell your boss he doesn't have to be concerned anymore."

Having to raise his voice so he could be heard through the door was exhausting him. He wanted nothing more than to just put his head on the table and pass out, but he was fully aware that he hadn't heard footsteps descending the stairs or the front door slamming. In fact, the landing in front of his door was still squeaking; she was shifting herself back and forth on the landing, waiting for him to open the door.

"Jesus," he muttered.

"What?" she called out from the other side.

"What the Hell do you want?"

"Please just let me in."

She's just not going to leave, is she? She wants to get a good almighty gander at what the cat puked up. I swear... if she even comes close to looking anywhere other than my eyes... she's going down those stairs ass first...

And that thought seemed to renew his strength, sending fresh blood pumping into his extremities. For the first time since he felt the first bite while chatting with Kitty, he smiled.

"Just a minute," he grunted as he hoisted himself onto his feet and made his way to the door. He ignored the great flares in his flesh as he steadied himself in front of the door and grasped the knob. As the door opened, he wrapped his fingers around the door to brace himself.

"Whatever you have to say, I'm in no mood for..."

And the fiercest, sharpest pain ripped through his hand. His arm reflexively jerked backwards and knocked him off balance. With a shocked scream, he toppled backwards and gasped to regain his wind. He might've passed out if it weren't for the fresh blood splashing his face. His right arm shook with pain as he held it in front of his face: blood was spurting from the stumps of where his first two fingers had been.

Eddie whimpered, unable to fully understand what was happening, and couldn't stop staring at his mangled hand until Jamyn strode into the room and slammed the door behind her. She stood over him, not surprised or curious about his wounds like everyone at the hospital had been, but fixing him with a cold stare and smiling as her jaws worked her infernal gum...

But she's not chewing gum... she wasn't chewing gum at the bar either!

After a minute of chewing, she swallowed and two short bones poked out of her smiling lips, which she nonchalantly spat across the floor.

"I don't like the bones," she said simply.

Eddie, lying on his back and trying to blink away the blood in his eyes, amazingly forgot about everything that had happened to him before that moment: his lashes and bites, his mangled nose and ear, the stitches holding his jugular together, even his missing fingers flew out of his head. All that there was in his world was the woman with flaming ginger hair standing in front of him, looking him up and down with blood-spittle dribbling from her mouth.

"What the Hell are..."

But he couldn't finish because Jamyn opened her mouth and seemingly bit the air in front of her. As her teeth came together, Eddie felt part of his cheek tear away. He screamed and turned his face into the carpet, soaking it through with blood. He started heaving with fear and forced himself to look back at her as she chewed and swallowed.

"They don't have a name for me yet, so I can't tell you. But I can tell you that you're just my type."

"Y-y-y-your t-t-t-t-t…"

"I like a lean man who's got a lot of strength in him; you can't imagine how good that tastes. Still you're quite a big guy, and I don't think I could finish you all up tonight, so you just might live to see tomorrow if you're lucky."

Eddie turned his face back into the carpet and shut his eyes tight, unable to stop shaking. "P-p-please, j-j-j-just leave me alone…"

"Look at me."

He kept his eyes shut and whimpered. Her voice got strangely low.

"Look at me or I'll bite your cock off!"

He turned his head towards the voice and opened his eyes. She was closer now, leaning over him, but there was no need for her to touch him. All she needed was to get a good look.

"You really have nice eyes," she said. "They're a delicacy."

Whatever Happened To Bobby?

(1996)
Hieronymus Scratch

His name was Dr. William Sendwin. He was fifty-two years old and had run a psychiatric clinic just outside of the city, in a spot where the trees grew a bit thicker and, except for the occasional truck speeding by, you could almost imagine yourself being miles away from whatever it was that put you in the clinic in the first place. Although Sendwin had founded the clinic himself, he'd decided to name it St. Peter's: simple, straightforward, to the point. When he'd first opened the clinic, he'd had a comforting image of St. Peter welcoming deserving souls through shining gates. That image had long since left him. By the end of his tenure, whenever he drove to work, he found himself thinking the same thing:

Welcome to St. Peter's, where I happily go every day to be crucified upside-down.

His portrait hung in the lobby and he would remark as he passed it every day that it was quite a fine and respectful rendition of the most highly-paid traffic cop in the world. And that was how Sendwin saw himself as he went through his day: settling disputes between opinionated young geniuses who spelled "Freud" with an "oi" and visiting the occasional patient to let them know that somebody in the building knew they were still alive.

In his youth, Sendwin had been fanatically devoted to his studies and his work. Consequently he never found time to find a wife or start a family, but that was quite alright since he liked living alone (and missed the solitary life ever since locking his new patient in the basement). His only real, close contact came from his best friend, Franklin Jones. He sometimes thought of Frank's family as his own, which is why he was shocked when, one day, Frank had called him to tell him that his oldest son, Charlie, had been torn to pieces in the woods behind the house by a wild animal.

He was further shocked to find out that that wasn't the real reason Frank had called him. The conversion went something like this:

Bill Sendwin: Oh Christ, Frank... I'll be right down... I'll... Christ...

Frank Jones: Bill, Shutup and let me finish! It's Bobby that I need to tell you about!

BS: Bobby? You mean he was there? Is he in shock?

FJ: No.

BS: I could come down there and see him. Would you like that?

FJ: Tonight, Bill. I'll bring him... to your house.

BS: That's fine... anything for you, man. How's Janet handling it? Is she...

FJ: You'll have to keep him there.

BS: You want him to stay the night while you two...

FJ: I want you to LOCK HIM UP!

BS: [pause] What the hell are you talking about?

FJ: You have to... I... I can't let anyone else see him.

BS: See him? Was he hurt? Did this animal that got Charlie do anything to...

FJ: I mean it, Bill. He has to be kept away from people. It has to be your house.

BS: But how long do you expect me to keep him here?

FJ: [pause] Until you cure him.

BS: Cure him of what?

[sounds of growling and slavering in the background]

Janet Jones: [in the background] Frank, he's breaking the ropes! What do I do?

FJ: In one hour, Bill.

JJ: [in the background] Bobby, no! NOOOO!

BS: Was that Janet? What the Hell is going...

FJ: Gotta go!

An hour later, Frank showed up with his youngest son at Sendwin's house.

The following day, Sendwin called the clinic and asked to speak with Dr. Trabor, a prissy Jungian who had his eye on Sendwin's post and was merely counting the days. He didn't have long to count. With Sendwin's secretary on the line to witness the whole exchange, Sendwin announced that he was resigning from St. Peter's and was handing the reigns over to Trabor, effective immediately.

The end of the conversation went something like this:

Bill Sendwin: You heard me, right?

Eric Trabor: I... I thought I did.

BS: Trust me, you did. Diana, did you hear it?

Diana Mills: [no response]

BS: Diana?

DM: I heard it, Doctor.

BS: You do recognize my voice, don't you?

DM: Yes.

BS: Then you'll instruct the staff that Dr. Trabor is to receive all the administrative power that was formally mine. They're to respect his decisions as they would respect mine… or not, as the case may be.

ET: Doctor…

BS: Just say "Thank you," Trabor, and hang up.

ET: But, what am I suppose to do about…

BS: Whatever you wish to do! Run the joint into the ground for all I care!

[Sound in background: banging and a low growl.]

DM: Doctor, are you alright?

BS: I'm fine.

ET: But what was that?

BS: Gotta go. Congrats, Trabor.

ET: But…

And now Sendwin, much thinner and older looking than he had been when he took that horrible call from his best friend, was standing on his porch keeping an eye out for the brown Saturn that he knew would be turning onto his street. He had gotten the call a couple of hours ago and they wouldn't be late for another ten minutes. He sat back into one of the four deck chairs and bit a piece off the paper cup he was holding, one newly emptied of a shot of his best scotch. He nervously chewed the paper and spat it to the deck.

Paper cups for scotch, he thought. He thought about the scotch, sitting on the kitchen counter in an old, plastic Coke bottle. He looked up and saw all the boarded-up windows along the side of the house. They hadn't survived the first day.

Nothing in the house made of glass had. Not after the first scream.

Sendwin was still looking up at the windows when he heard the car pulling up. He knew it was Frank's; Sendwin's street was a private way and only those who had business with him turned onto his street.

The car pulled into the driveway and Frank, tired, gray and wearing jeans and a pullover, got out. The woman that Frank said would be with him got out on the other side. She was in her thirties, neatly dressed, and seemed uncertain as she stepped out of the car.

Sendwin nodded to the pair and then was suddenly on his feet and waving his arms as he saw both of them about to slam the car doors.

Frank saw and tapped the roof of the car, catching Rebecca's attention just in time.

"What?" she asked.

"I think that..." Frank looked up at Sendwin, who was nodding fervently. "Yes, I guess he's sleeping."

Frank gently closed his door, so gently that it was barely closed at all. Rebecca looked around, decided that the neighborhood (*some neighborhood... one house*) was safe enough to leave a barely secured car, and did the same.

The two of them walked up to the porch, walking on the grass instead of the path. Frank winced a bit as the stairs to the porch made a slight creek as he ascended them. Frank and the doctor nodded sadly to each other. Rebecca hung back, seeing Frank say a few words and then lean his head down, which bobbed forward with sobs. The doctor put his arms around him to comfort him.

They're talking about his wife, Rebecca guessed correctly. On the drive there, Mr. Jones had related in a dead and distant voice what she had finally decided to do that morning. At the time, he sounded dulled by the shock of it all. Seeing his old friend had apparently brought him back to the heart of the misery.

The doctor let his friend go and the exhausted and saddened man fell quietly into a nearby deckchair, as if every last bit of his strength was expelled just getting to that spot. Rebecca had a feeling that she might have to take a cab back into the city. The doctor quietly approached Rebecca and walked past her, motioning with his head for her to follow.

The two scuffled their way from the house. When they were twenty feet away, the doctor turned and took a good look at her for the first time. Though he knew she was older, her lithe body made her look like she was still in her mid-twenties, except the expression on her face betrayed her actual age. Still, she was pretty and the much-older and balding Sendwin thought for a moment about some of the things he'd given up to achieve the privilege of founding a clinic he no longer cared about.

He leaned towards her and whispered. "Your name escapes me."

"Rebecca Dyne. Mr. Jones told me who you are."

"Did he?"

"He said you were looking after his son."

"Did he tell you why?"

Rebecca hesitated, but not because she wasn't sure she could trust the doctor. She still wasn't sure that she believed what Mr. Jones had told her a few days before on the phone, when she'd answered the ring and heard the voice of a desperate man saying, "I read what you wrote and I know what you did." Something in his voice had told her not to hang up, that there was more on the other end of the line than just a crank. Maybe it was part of her artistic temperament that allowed her to listen to Mr. Jones's obviously lunatic story; there definitely *was* a story in here somewhere, something that could be embellished and turned into another best-seller. Things like what Mr. Jones described just didn't happen except in her books. In fact, what he'd described *had* happened in one of her very own stories quite recently.

"I'm a writer… you've probably never heard of me…"

"Not until this morning, no."

"About eight months ago, I published a short story called 'IT' in 'Alfred Hitchcock'… I've published a couple of novels too…"

"If you're looking to impress me, young lady, I'm not interested…"

"Don't call me 'Young Lady.' I'm not your daughter!"

Sendwin bit his lip and reminded himself that this woman had only just joined the rollercoaster that was the Bobby Jones Experience. He nodded.

"When did you first hear from Frank?"

"Earlier this week. He told me about something that happened to his children; he said one of them had killed the other and that, after the initial shock wore off, he remembered reading the story a few months earlier and decided that I was to blame. He said I got the names right and everything."

"And what's your story about?" Sendwin guessed what the answer was, but he wanted to hear Ms. Dyne say it. She looked down at the grass before she spoke.

"A little boy is playing Hide 'n Seek and is sick of being It all the time. After his brother's friends tease him, he gets so frustrated that he…"

She dug a piece of Sendwin's grass out of the ground with the toe of her shoe before answering.

"…he turns into a werewolf."

"And then what?"

"And then nothing. It just ends with the kid walking into the forest, looking for his brother's friends."

"To kill them?"

She didn't know why she felt so ashamed to be relating a tale that she'd been so proud to have thought of only a year before. "I write all kinds of stuff… I don't always do fantasy… but I was thinking about how kids must feel after being bullied and how much they wish they had the power to…"

"… to kill."

"… to pay them back, that's all."

Sendwin took a deep breath. "That's a hell of way to pay back, don't you think?"

She wanted to yell at the doctor and tell him to stop looking at her like she was some sort of incubus risen from the pit of Hell. She looked away and found herself captured by the figure of Frank Jones, still sitting on the porch, the figure of a broken and defeated man. "Look, if you believe that this kid…"

"Bobby, just like in your story, remember?"

"…yeah, read what I wrote and was inspired to hurt his brother and his friends, all I can say is that my work isn't meant for young readers and I certainly don't encourage anyone to solve their problems through violence. Now whatever it is you and Mr. Jones have to show me…"

"Frank won't be coming in," Sendwin said with authority. "Even if he wanted to, I wouldn't let him."

Rebecca just stared at Dr. Sendwin while he took a moment to make a decision. He kept shaking his head, but apparently decided to carry on anyway.

"Aw, Hell. Look, you'll do everything I tell you to do, understand?" If Dr. Sendwin ever had a bedside manner, it was long eroded from the time spent caring for his one, special patient. "You'll be my shadow until I say otherwise. You'll talk when I tell you to talk. You'll leave when I tell you to leave. Any deviations from this and…"

"Yes, and?" Rebecca never liked being preached to and she was questioning why she'd allowed herself to be talked into coming here in the first place; her agent had warned her to let him call a lawyer in case Mr. Jones decided to get litigious. "Stay away from the goons," he always told her, "They'll always think you were writing about them.

These people are sad and delusional. Don't let them get inside your head." But the story that Mr. Jones had told her on the phone was too incredible and he didn't sound as if he wanted to sue her.

He sounded like he was looking for understanding.

However Dr. Sendwin, with his sleepless eyes and ethanol breath, seemed to want nothing more than to creep her out.

"And I just might let you stay in there with him."

* * *

The door to the cellar was locked.

And barred.

And chained.

The fortifications were all new compared to the door to which they had been affixed. Rebecca had trouble taking her eyes from them when the doctor tapped her on the shoulder. She turned and saw the man there with his hand out. In his palm was a set of earplugs.

"You keep an seven year-old child in here? You can't *do* that! I could turn around right now and bring the cops back here!" Rebecca didn't realize that she was whispering her threat to the doctor. Whatever it was he was afraid of, real or imagined, it was contagious.

"Put these in," he whispered hoarsely, ignoring her protests.

Rebecca grasped them in an uncertain hand and hesitated.

"How will I hear you?"

"I'll have my hand on your arm at all times. When I pull you back to the door that means we're leaving… as fast as possible. Can you remember that?"

Rebecca smirked and plugged one ear. "What will he be doing

when we go in?"

"Dozing, I think. I don't think it ever fully sleeps. Its instincts for survival are wound pretty tightly."

"What have you done to him?"

Sendwin looked at her with growing impatience. "It doesn't completely understand what has happened to it and it reacts accordingly."

"Doesn't *completely* understand? Jesus, Doctor, a traumatized boy needs to be in a hospital. I shouldn't think you'd need to be told…"

Sendwin pulled his arm away and reached for the first lock. "You'd better put that other plug in before…"

Rebecca placed her hand on Sendwin's one last time. "Does he at least get decent food?"

Sendwin looked up and considered for a moment.

"You and I would consider the food decent; I have a feeling that It wants something else."

Rebecca plugged up her other ear. She couldn't hear Sendwin undo the locks that held the door tight on its frame, but she wouldn't have heard much even without the earplugs: Sendwin was adept at unlocking the door without making a sound. Likewise, the hinges were silent. The absence of sound only succeeded in making Rebecca more nervous, that and the fact that the doctor reached into the corner and pulled out a heavy baseball bat, which he gripped steadily and tightly in his right hand. His left hand also fixed itself hard on something solid - Rebecca's shoulder. Sendwin pulled his guest into the doorway.

Rebecca, forgetting about the earplugs, was about to ask about the bat when her eyes caught sight of the back of the cellar door; the heavy wood was crisscrossed with scars and scratches.

Rebecca got one last look at the doctor's face, pinched and steeled against the fury of his young patient, before she was completely pulled into the darkness.

She was pulled quickly down the crumbling stones steps and had to work to keep from stumbling. Near the bottom, she missed a step and her hand flailed to the wall, finding the familiar and comforting shape of a light switch under her palm. Instinctively, her fingers flipped the switch. But no light came on: Sendwin had monkeyed with the bulbs long before. There was no light, not even from the top of the stairs because Sendwin had closed the door behind them. Rebecca felt herself dragged through the darkness, impulsively fighting the clutching hand that held her. She choked on musty air and kicked bits of plaster lying on the floor out of her way.

What the Hell am I doing here? I must be insane! This guy has a bat, we're in the dark, and I can't even remember what his first name is! Did he hypnotize me or something? How could I have let myself in for something so stupid? Sweet Jesus, I'm never going to see my Dad or any of my friends again...

And suddenly, there was light in Rebecca's eyes.

Sendwin, his hand still clutched to Rebecca's shoulder, was standing in front of her. The bat was temporarily out of the doctor's hand and laying at his feet. He was instead extending his hand towards the source of the light, a flashlight hanging on a wire from the ceiling. He turned the beam towards himself, and Rebecca blinked as the light flashed into her eyes for a moment.

Now that there was light and she could see the bat lying on the floor, Rebecca took a step backwards, feeling the time was right to turn this crazy situation back to her favor. Sendwin held her fast, but she felt strong enough (and scared enough) to break free.

Then he suddenly swung the light away.

The beam spotlighted pieces of the empty room before them. Rebecca guessed from what little she could see that it had once been a den, but the comforts of quiet Sundays spent in front of the TV had been removed. Only patches of homey tan wallpaper were caught in the flashlight's beam.

Only patches. The rest had been torn away.

Clawed away.

And then, very faintly through the earplugs, she heard a heavy chain dragged along the floor.

Sendwin pointed the beam of light into the corner and Rebecca saw the chain for a brief moment. One moment it was lying coiled but lightly being dragged out, the next it was pulled taut - just as the small spotlight was filled with something.

Rebecca tried to jump back, but her ankles tangled and she fell down hard. She let out a strangled "oof" as her breath was knocked out of her. Something in her head decompressed and suddenly there was clear sound on her left side. She reached up to her ear.

The earplug was gone.

Instinctively, she flailed around the floor with her hands as her eyes, so recently trying to adjust to the single beam of light, were now combating with the darkness. She didn't know why the earplug was so important, but it didn't matter now. Her hands slapped at the hard floor, coming up empty each time.

She clearly heard the chain straining with force.

She heard tortured breathing, becoming raspy and almost growling...

That's not me.

The light was suddenly on her and she looked up to see that the doctor had swung it back, presumably to help her find the earplug. But all Rebecca could think of in that one moment was that the thing at the end of the chain could see her.

"Get that thing off me," she shouted. The last words were cut off by loud aggravated barking. They were getting louder and higher in pitch.

"Too late," she heard the doctor shout above the barks. "Just cover your ears! Hurry!"

And the growling and barking became a tortured moan, getting higher and higher. Tears squirted out of Rebecca's eyes. Just as the thing took a deep breath, Rebecca clapped her hand tightly over her left ear.

Sendwin swung the light back to whatever it was that was in front of them. Rebecca looked up into the spotlight and saw something hairy raise its head to the ceiling. It closed its eyes in anticipation and Rebecca did the same.

Here... it... comes!

And the creature's howl filled the room, so loud that it pierced into Rebecca's blocked ears and drilled into her brain. She rolled over, hoping to find something she could bury her head in, but only found the hard floor. Warm liquid flowed onto her tongue as she realized only dimly that she'd bitten through her bottom lip.

It hurts, it hurts, it hurts, it hurts...

Something hit the floor next to her and Rebecca knew, but didn't much care, that the doctor had joined her. An image of the roof flying off the house flooded her mind. Every hair in her scalp seemed to vibrate painfully with the drawn-out howl and, as the blood shot into her brain, she counted slowly backwards from ten, knowing that the top of her head would explode when she reached zero.

8... 7... 6... 5... 4... 3...

And with a hoarse bark, it was over.

Rebecca forced herself to open her eyes once the pounding in her head stopped. Slowly, her eyes focused on the scene before her: the mostly dark palette that was the room, the semi-bright flickering spot that swayed and cut through the blackness

(*Into the deep... the color is black*)

and caught in its weakening glare a figure with its head down, secured by the chain, with a steel collar affixed around its neck.

A figure covered with hair taking the deepest of breaths.

...exhausted... just like us...

Rebecca saw a figure about to collapse out of the spot of the flashlight. With its head down and its body panting in sad weariness, any impulse that Rebecca felt to be scared drifted away. Instead, she looked at the figure with course hair growing out of every pore, which stood barely five feet in height and made sounds that could be confused as either sobbing or low growls.

Its ears were pointed.

Rebecca forced herself to keep looking.

It lifted its head and turned its mouth into something that could be easily mistaken for a smile, pointed teeth glistening. Rebecca could see that it was only an expression of an animal, a grin of savagery. The human muscles had receded, leaving only the basic scowl of the primitive behind. The face was both young and old. The eyes reared forward and locked onto Rebecca's face. It breathed out great horrid fumes that billowed in her face and made her gag. And through it all, she couldn't bring herself to turn away from the face of the scared child that dwelt behind it all.

It was Bobby's face, a face she'd never seen except in her imagination; it quivered and soundlessly asked how much longer it would have to suffer.

I couldn't help it… I didn't want to hurt anybody.

Beneath the fur and teeth was the face of the boy, who didn't understand anything that was going on anymore than Rebecca or the doctor did.

Only knowing that he had to bite.

He had to eat.

He had to howl.

Rebecca felt her stomach roll over with the stench of the creature's breath, but couldn't bring herself to move away. She would've stayed there forever if the light from the entrance door opening hadn't caught her attention.

"Bobby? Are you down here?"

Both Rebecca and the doctor followed the sound of the cracked voice to the light at the end of the hall. Rebecca was surprised to see that the length of hallway that she'd walked wasn't as long as she'd thought it had been in the pitch dark. A square of light shone behind them and a human shadow came closer, swaying back and forth as it made its way towards them.

"Frank, get back upstairs!"

Rebecca turned back to the creature and saw it strain at its chain with a renewed strength. The spot from the flashlight drifted across its sniffing and expectant nose.

Snout! That's a snout if ever I saw one!

"Bobby, it's me! It's Daddy. I'm not angry anymore. I swear I'm not." Jones was nearly upon the pair and Rebecca felt Sendwin moving to block the despondent man's path.

"Frank, get back upstairs! I told you…"

"You've had enough time to cure him." The scuffle that Rebecca heard going on a few feet from her was both intense and brief. Footsteps continued past her into the creature's chamber. "Bobby, I'm not angry anymore."

"Frank!" Sendwin called out to Jones just as his body eclipsed the beam of the flashlight. Rebecca tried to look past the bereaved man and saw only a sickly, hairy smile full of teeth.

"Bobby, is that you?"

There was a low, expectant growl. Rebecca could hear it

inhumanly waiting for the perfect moment.

Sendwin's hand swatted against her shoulder.

"Get the Hell out of here!"

Frank Jones's cracked voice was getting fainter as he stalked deeper into what would be his last foray into fatherhood.

"Bobby…"

And with the sound of the roar and the heavy pounce that followed, Rebecca found the energy to jump up and run for the open door at the end of the hall. When she reached the stairs, she stomped on them heavily as she climbed them, hoping to drown out the sounds: the sounds of Jones screaming, the sound of Sendwin calling out in vain to his friend, the sound of the creature roaring in delight, the sound of the chain scraping along the floor and the sickening, wet tearing that she did not want to even think about.

But no matter how fast she ran he couldn't escape the horrible sound of her own screams.

* * *

"You'll have to take the car and ditch it somewhere."

"Excuse me?"

"The police will want to know what happened to him. They can't come here. He left his jacket out here; the keys are probably in the pocket."

The two of them were sitting on the front porch, sipping scotch out of paper cups. The plastic coke bottle that held the brown liquor sat between them, seriously depleted during the last half hour, although Rebecca didn't feel in the least bit tipsy. In fact, she'd felt drunker in that highly aware moment when she'd burst out of the house and nearly screamed for help, stopping herself only when she looked around and remembered that Dr. Sendwin had no neighbors.

There comes a point in life when Sobriety becomes an unnatural state.

"Maybe..." she said, pouring herself another hit from the bottle, "...maybe it would be better if you..."

The doctor looked up at her and finished her thought. "...put it out of my misery?"

Something about his tone bothered her, a snooty and sarcastic dismissal. "What about *its* misery?"

"You think I haven't thought about that?"

"But what are you *doing* about it? I suppose you've also thought about what happens if it gets you one day. What's to keep it from escaping? I know you sit up in your room all night, drinking this shit, listening to it skulk around in the basement and convince yourself that it's human, but what are you gonna *do* about it?"

He scowled at her and Rebecca could tell that she would've been wearing his drink on her face had he not wanted to waste it. She sat back and took another sip, letting him stomach her words.

Very slowly, he said, "This wasn't *my* fault."

"You saying it's mine?"

"You told me yourself you had a character named 'Bobby' who..."

"Stephen King had a car named 'Christine' but I haven't seen any '57 Plymouth Furies driving down the street on their own, have you?"

"We're not talking about *FUCKING STEPHEN KING*," he shouted, not listening to the echoing growl coming from inside the house. "We're talking about my godson and what's happened to him!"

Rebecca was on her feet. "I'm still not convinced that that thing in there was once human! You could have some weird wild animal chained up in there!"

"How many wolves have you seen that can walk upright?"

"I'm not convinced!" she shouted, mostly to drown out the doubts that were assailing her, and she stomped off for the car, only to stop midway when she realized it wasn't her car. She made a fist and pounded her thigh when it occurred to her that the owner of the car was apparently not going to be giving her a ride back anytime in the near future. Sheepishly, she turned back to the porch; Sendwin had Mr. Jones's jacket in his hand and was going through the pockets.

"I'm calling a cab," she shouted back to him before reaching in her pocket for her cellphone.

Sendwin slumped. "Can't you just get the car out of here? I can't just leave Bobby here on his own. Please, Ms. Dyne!" But Rebecca put her finger in her other ear and was hurrying off to the edge of the driveway.

With the last person in the world who knew what he had locked up in his house running away from him, something inside of him breached. "You think it's easy? You're not here in the middle of the night when it whimpers, when I can almost hear Bobby's voice coming back, when that monster's jaw is almost able to form words! *I can hear him calling me! I CAN HEAR HIM! DON'T LEAVE, MS. DYNE! WHY*

IS THIS HAPPENING?"

She walked down to the corner and waited ten minutes for the cab to arrive. She could still hear the doctor shouting for her to come back, but she knew he wouldn't leave his post.

It wouldn't be safe.

When the cab arrived, she closed the door quickly so that the driver wouldn't hear the shouting, which had become mixed with hysterical pleas.

"Where to, lady?"

Rebecca needed to go someplace quiet to think; it wasn't difficult to come up with the perfect place.

"Do you know where the Memorial Café is?"

Mommy And The Midnight Caller

(1975)
Little Ronnie

Little Ronnie huddled in the cramped darkness, smelling the mothballs stuffed into Mommy's tattered, woolly coat and prayed. He prayed very hard and very quietly. He had to pray hard because the Holy Father had no mercy for wicked little boys like him. He had to pray quietly because Mommy said only then would his prayer be considered genuine.

Years before, she'd taught little Ronnie what words to use.

My Holy Father, forgive me for being unworthy.

My Holy Father, forgive me for being unwashed.

My Holy Father, forgive me for being vile.

My Holy Father, forgive me for being disgusting.

And on and on through all thirty-nine ("One for each of the lashes inflicted on our Lord," Mommy reminded him) entreaties, each one worse than the last.

...forgive me for being...

...forgive me for...

...forgive me...

...forgive...

After thirty-eight pleas, the last always came out in a choked whisper.

My Holy Father, forgive me for being Ronnie Wilson.

And after reflecting upon this last horrible offense against the Holy Father, he would start again from the beginning. And over and over again until Mommy let him out.

And that's how it had been for the longest time until he came up with his own, even more heartfelt prayer. It came out of his mouth in spitting whispers.

"My Holy Father, kill Mommy for me, please. I promise I'll never ask for anything else. I'll give you everything I have, but please, please, please kill Mommy."

He'd say it over and over again in the confines of the closet when he heard Mommy's footsteps disappear down the hall, when he was absolutely certain that her ear was no longer pressed against the door. Still, even when Mommy's prying ears were far away, little Ronnie couldn't allow himself to become too carried away with his new prayer. He had to keep his wits about him, had to keep his ears finely tuned.

Sometimes, Mommy would creep back to the closet door and lightly press her ear against it.

Once, Mommy had heard little Ronnie snoring and smiled because she knew the pot of water boiling on the stove would not go to waste.

So little Ronnie prayed sharply and quietly, and listened for Mommy. Once, he thought he heard the creak of Mommy's step on the floorboard just outside the room. The darkness had intensified his hearing and his ears tuned minutely to the warning signal that he knew so well: the ball of Mommy's foot balancing neatly on the floorboard.

Nothing.

So intensely was little Ronnie listening for Mommy's steps that he nearly didn't feel the tiny brushing against his knee. Scared, he drew back as much as the cramped closet would let him. His eyes darted but saw nothing in the dark. He breathed deeply in large gasps as he stared and looked harder.

Slowly, he made out a shape in the darkness. There, on his right, something scuttled close to the wall.

Ronnie pressed himself closer to the closet door, trying not to scream. The thing on the floor was small, but Ronnie imagined that Mr. Scratch (as Mommy referred to him) might be small, just small enough to creep into the closet unseen to a shivering, penitent boy. Then it would get much bigger. Then it would...

The outlines around the creature finally came together in the darkness. Ronnie peered deep and saw what had scared him.

A lizard.

Small, dark (green or gray probably, he thought) and staring up at him like a tiny, silent Kermit the Frog.

Ronnie giggled then covered his mouth tightly so that Mommy wouldn't hear.

Ronnie lowered his hand and was pleased to feel the lizard's tiny feet climbing onto his palm. It was light and alive. Ronnie slowly lifted the creature and brought it very near his face. It didn't scamper when it felt itself being lifted. It didn't try to jump to the floor and find whatever hole it came from to escape. It sat there and looked at him.

Hi-Ho.

It's tongue quickly leapt out and back in again.

Ronnie's tongue did the same.

The two of them stood looking at each other, tongues shooting in and out almost in unison.

"I can't hear you in there!"

It was Mommy. Her stocking foot had lightly skipped over the squeaky floorboard and Ronnie could hear her voice coming from just beyond the door. The lizard twitched in his hand and looked towards the disturbance. Ronnie immediately started reciting the litany of penance.

My Holy Father, forgive me for being unworthy.

My Holy Father, forgive me for being unwashed.

My Holy Father, forgive me for being vile.

My Holy Father, forgive me for being disgusting.

The doorknob moved slightly. Ronnie shrank against the corner of the closet and the prayer spilled out of his mouth faster than he could control it.

My Holy Father forgive me for being dirtyMyHolyFather, forgivemeforbeingthoughtless MyHolyFatherforgivemeforbeingsinful-MyHolyFatherforgivemeforbeingaboy...

The pressure on the doorknob loosened. The floorboard creaked. Mommy's footsteps disappeared into the apartment. While Ronnie tried to relax again, there was another sound following Mommy's departure. Soft but firm.

Thud... thud... thud... thud... thud...

Strong wood lightly falling into the palm of a hand.

Mommy was letting a baseball bat fall lightly into her hand. Over and over. Just so he could hear the sound. Just to let him know that she had it ready. If she were to catch him sinning one more time during his penance…

"My Holy Father, kill Mommy for me, please. I promise I'll never ask for anything else. I'll give you everything I have, but please, please, please kill Mommy. Kill her, kill her, kill her, kill her, kill her…"

And that's when he felt his little visitor jump up and scamper out of his palm. Ronnie made a blind wave in the air to catch him, afraid of being left. He felt only the barest touch of the lizard's tail as it fell. The lizard landed with the lightest of steps and shot like bullet through a small hole in the back wall.

Ronnie leaned over further, getting his head down to the level of the floor, one open eye peering, but the lizard was gone. Into the deep.

Ronnie looked deeper into the hole.

The color is Black.

He sat up sharply. Where had that come from? A voice inside his head had spoken it, but he'd never heard the voice before. It sounded gruff and secretive.

Into the deep… the color is Black.

Mommy was right, Ronnie thought. I've sinned and sinned and sinned and now Mr. Scratch is talking to me. Telling me riddles. He's inside my head!

Ronnie continued the prayer Mommy had taught him. His voice was louder and stronger; it was the only way he could think of to cast out the demon of the lizard hole.

* * *

Little Ronnie lay in bed that night unable to sleep because he was so thankful of many things: thankful that he had not sinned during the rest of his penance (or during the rest of the day, for that matter), thankful that Mommy had not discovered some new sin that he was committing without knowing it and thus earn him another trip to the penance chamber, thankful that Mommy had not hidden anything hard or sharp in his mash potatoes again to teach him the lesson that evil was lurking in even the most innocent of places.

And especially, he was thankful that the voice in his head had gone away.

Ronnie sank into his bed, the darkness as comforting as the pillow cradling his head and the warm blanket that Mommy had made for him years ago, long before she had "found the Father," as she called it. Back then things had been different. He supposed things hadn't actually been better; how could they have been with the Father absent from their lives? Things just seemed better and Mommy had said it had all been an illusion that the Devil had spun around them, tricking them, making them think they were happy, contented and blessed.

Mommy had explained it all.

Now, we're blessed. Someday, perhaps in the next world, we'll be happy and contented. But at least we're blessed. We didn't have anything before. You must never forget that. We're blessed now.

And even though the Holy Father had no mercy ("Why should God have mercy for anyone, especially you," Mommy had said), that was alright, because being blessed was all that mattered.

Ronnie lay on his bed, letting his thoughts take him back to what a sinner he used to be. He even winced when he remembered the time he'd kicked Mommy in the knee when he wouldn't settle down while watching the scary movie.

He'd been a horrible, little demon back then, as bad as Mr. Scratch himself.

(*I'm blessed, now*)

He missed seeing those scary movies with all the gooshy parts.

(*No, those movies were evil. I don't miss them. I'm blessed, now.*)

He missed the other kids in the neighborhood and stickball on Saturdays.

(*Those kids never walked with the Father. They were leading me into the pit one pitch at a time. I'm blessed, now.*)

He missed...

(*I'm blessed, now.*)

There was a sound.

Ronnie heard it but couldn't bring himself to sit up. His heart hammered. All thoughts of his and Mommy's blessed state flew away as the sound came again.

Four quick stomps and a long, sickening slither.

It was coming down the hallway, coming closer to his bedroom door with every step. Four feet and...

(*But... I'm blessed! Mommy said so! I'm blessed!*)

...and a tail were coming down the hallway.

Ronnie jumped out of bed and crouched down behind the side

that was furthest from the door. Along the outside of the wall, something scraped. There was a crash and clatter that made him cower further behind the bed.

That was the table with the lamp, he thought as the steps came closer. It hit the table with it's...

(*No, we're blessed, blessed, BLESSED!*)

It hit the table with its tail.

"Ronnie, what was that?"

Mommy's voice, calling from the bedroom further down the hall. She'd been sleeping only a moment before, but there was none of that in her voice now. The same clarity and anger was unmistakable, even at two in the morning.

"Ronnie, did you break something?"

The sound was right outside his door. Four stomps and a slither. Four feet and a tail. Ronnie whimpered as he clutched the mattress tightly.

"Ronnie, you know what happens to wicked, sinful boys who get up in the middle of the night?"

The sound kept moving past his door, further down the hallway, heading towards...

And then Ronnie not only remembered his secret prayer from earlier that day, but who had heard it. In a flash, he finally realized what was in the hallway. He knew what was heading towards Mommy.

"Mommy," he cried out, "Lock the door! Put something in front of it! It's coming for you!"

"Young man, I've had just about..."

And then her voice stopped dead as four more stomps echoed through the hall.

Silence.

Something was deciding.

"Ronnie?"

The words were out of his mouth before he could stop them. "I didn't mean to do it, Mommy! I just…"

And then there was the crash of wood splintering, the horrible scream, and the four stomps and slithering against the carpet, quicker since it had found its prey.

Ronnie dove under the bed, dragging half the sheets with him. Mommy's screaming continued, blasting out the inside of his head.

CRASH! Tinkle… tinkle…

Those are Mommy's bottles of perfume. Its tail must've…

SMASH!

The mirror above the bureau.

And then Ronnie heard Mommy's last coherent cry.

"Stop! In the name of the Father! You dare not come closer! You dare not…"

And then Ronnie's world exploded into a series of screams and crashes.

* * *

When little Ronnie slowly crawled out from under his bed the next morning, all he heard was the singing of a few birds outside his window. The song did not warm him, nor did the beautiful ray of sunshine coming through the window. He only stood there and shivered

in its light. Then he realized that he would never have been able to hear
the birds if the creature were still stomping and crashing through the
hallway.

It's gone!

He ran to the door and threw it opened, looking to see the trail of
destruction that it had left.

There was none.

Ronnie stepped into the middle of the hallway and spun around,
taking in every detail. Each picture was hung straight on its nail, just as
they were the day before. He'd imagined scraped-off wallpaper, cracks
and holes in the walls and piles of dusty plaster. Everything was in
order.

He caught sight of the little table that stood between his bedroom
door and the living room, the one that the creature's tail had smashed as
it made its way down the hall. It stood perfectly stable and polished.
The lamp that he had heard crashing against the wall sat unbroken on it,
its ugly, green lampshade free of dust as it was the day before.

He turned and wasn't sure if he should be surprised that
Mommy's bedroom door stood closed on its hinges when it should have
been a smashed pile of splinters.

But I heard it, he thought as he went to the door and pushed it
open. He looked around and everything was in its place. The bottles of
perfume stood exactly where they always had. The huge mirror stood
tall and proud on its support. The bed was neatly made, the sheets and
comforter stretched across the mattress without a wrinkle. Everything
was where it should be and everything was immaculate.

Mommy was the only thing that wasn't where she should have been. The room was empty.

"Looking for me?"

The voice came from behind him and he spun around. Despite all the evidence to the contrary, Ronnie knew that whatever it was that happened the night before was no dream when he got a look at Mommy. Although her voice was strong, she was shaking and her eyes were darting all over the area, as if both on the lookout for something and deadly afraid that she might actually find it. Her hair looked as if she had her finger stuck in an electrical socket. One hand was pressed against the wall, trying to steady herself and keep her on her feet.

"What… what happened to…" and he trailed away.

"What happened to *what*?" she screamed, her voice cracking. "Get into the penance chamber!"

"But I didn't…"

"You *did*! You *did* do it! You sent that thing to me! I always knew you were evil! Pure, black evil. From the moment you came out of me!"

Ronnie had to grip the closet door to keep from falling.

"…how much of your salvation did you promise to conjure up that…"

A key inside his head finally turned, and he knew at last what to do.

"You did it!"

"*Yes, I did it!*" Ronnie screamed. "And I'll do it again and you can't stop me!"

Mommy stepped back, stumbled against her own slippers, and fell to the floor. Her eyes never left her son and her already pale face turned the color of fresh chalk.

"And don't think you can tell anybody about it! Nobody else heard it last night and nothing's changed! They'd never believe you! They'd lock you up and then I'd be free of you forever!"

Mommy cowered on the floor, drawing her arms around her knees. "Evil," she said in a voice that had no force to it.

"*You* get into the penance chamber!"

"...blackest evil..."

"Go or I'll send it after you again!"

"...evil..."

"GO!" Ronnie's voice echoed even louder than the swishing of the creature's tail the night before.

And Mommy slowly rose from the floor and, like a woman possessed, walked into her son's room. Ronnie looked through his open bedroom door as she silently walked into his closet and shut the door behind her.

Ronnie went to the kitchen and fixed himself a bowl of cornflakes, pouring a few scoops of fudge syrup on it for good measure. He ate three bowls while he waited for the pan of water he placed on the stove to come to a boil.

The only sound in the apartment came from his crunching teeth and the hiss of the boiling water. He heard nothing from the woman in his closet. A brief thought about Mommy's Mr. Scratch occurred to him, but he didn't let it bother him; in fact, he felt warmed by the idea that he'd beaten Mommy with the thing that she feared the most.

Little Ronnie threw his bowl into the sink, smiling as he heard it break. He walked to the window and looked out at the world filled with sunshine before him. He felt better than he had in quite a while.

He wasn't exactly sure what he would do with his new-found power.

But he would think of something.

Teach Yourself Satanism

(2001)
Hieronymus Scratch

Seven months before she got a job behind the counter at the Memorial Café, Sophie Wynosky sold her soul to the Devil... or at least to the closest thing to the Devil that she could get her hands on.

This was not a move that she took lightly (at two-hundred and thirty-six pounds, there was very little that she could take lightly, even if she wanted to), but it was the only move she felt she could take in the wake of her rejection from the Wiccans.

How can they not believe in Satan, she'd thought. At least Christians gave you a choice.

She never thought of herself as evil, per se. After all, she wasn't out slaughtering millions of Jews, was she? That was unadulterated evil, make no mistake about it. She held no interest in the cracking of the fragile skulls of those who didn't bow down to whatever it was she chose to believe in that week. She wasn't evil. In the words of her psychologist (written in the medical file that she probably shouldn't have stolen and taken a quick peek through), she just found evil...

Interesting.

Well, didn't everybody?

So, when the Wiccan door slammed shut in her face, Sophie

decided to sell her soul to the Devil. All she had to do was find him and figure out the actual machinations for such a business deal.

The second part of her task didn't seem to present too much of a problem to her. Make a pledge and you're in. And blood should be involved somehow, shouldn't there? Blood and some type of sacrifice. That's how it was always done in the movies.

Finding Satan was another matter entirely. Evil was all around, but in different quantities. Sophie suspected that choosing any old hub of evil just wouldn't do, so conducting a Satanic ceremony in front of Mr. Pickney down at the local butcher shop, who overcharged and probably mixed horsemeat in with the prime rib, would probably be a complete waste of time.

Still, she didn't have the money to fly to Washington D.C. and pick out a Senator to damn herself to so she resolved to sell her soul to the most evil thing within her limited radius of existence.

And so it came to pass that on March 7th, 2000, eighteen year-old Sophie Wynoski sold her soul to a photograph of Rush Limbaugh.

It was a simple and thoroughly confusing ceremony: held in the darkened confines of her padlocked bedroom while her mother believed she was doing her homework. The lights were out and three black candles, bought at an occult shop across town called "Chock Full Of Ghoulies," were flickering in the darkness. Sophie had undressed and sat cross-legged (as best she could manage) on the floor in front of the photo, trying to ignore the ache in her back.

Sitting in front of her, along with the photo, were a kitchen knife, a dead mouse caught in a mousetrap, and a bag of snuff.

The soundtrack to "The Exorcist" was playing just loud enough to create the proper atmosphere (and to keep from alerting her mother as to what was going on). Sophie began reciting strange syllables softly. Although she knew she was just making it all up, she hoped that the atmosphere was causing her to tap into some primal evil circuit so that her gobbledygook would make some degree of sense to some Dark Father somewhere.

Sophie gingerly lifted the mousetrap, the mouse swaying limply in its jaws, and quietly chanted a bit more gibberish. She slowly lifted the wire clamp and released the dead mouse from the trap, where it fell with a soft plop onto Limbaugh's face. A few drops of blood spattered in a tiny radius around the mouse's body.

Sophie then picked up the bag of snuff and opened it. She remembered reading somewhere about an old superstition about how a sneeze was the release of one's soul. In a very ceremonial and flourishing way, she reached into the bag, produced a very large wad of powdery tobacco, and sniffed the whole thing into her nose. Never having tried snuff before, she had no idea what would happen next, but the reaction was immediate. The room shook with a mighty "HAAAAHT-CHOOOOO" as wet snuff went flying into the image of Limbaugh's face and covered the mouse's corpse.

After six more sneezes (and grateful that her mother, three rooms away, did not respond with a blessing as that would have ruined the whole demonic atmosphere), Sophie took the knife and sliced open the pad of her left index finger without flinching. The pain sent a beautiful blue ark of lightning into her brain and she knew that she wasn't making any mistakes. She held her finger over Limbaugh's face and squeezed two drops of blood perfectly into each of his eyes, turning him into a little smiling imp with red pupils. Pleased with her handiwork, she used a bit more blood to draw horns on his bald head.

She knew that the only way to properly complete the ceremony was to burn the entire mound of gruesome relics to ashes, but she couldn't take the chance of setting fire to her bedroom. Sophie instead crumpled the whole package up and flushed it down the toilet.

As the remains of Limbaugh, mouse, snot and blood went to their watery grave, Sophie went back into her room, jumped onto the bed and waited for something mystical and chilling to happen.

To her surprise, nothing did.

Subtle guy, she thought.

That didn't stop her from considering herself a bride of Satan, so she decided that she'd better start acting like one. To that end, Sophie assumed an all-black wardrobe which included a hoodie (which refused to be zipped up over her massive chest), black jackboots and makeup to give her a dark, zombified look. She even wrapped a dog collar around her neck to show the world that she was Satan's mutt.

As a bride of Satan, Sophie figured she needed a wedding ring. This was not a problem as her mother had removed hers in the wake of a bitter divorce and left it in an ashtray by her bedside. Sophie's mother, exhausted from waiting on big smelly truckers at the route 95 pit stop all day, never noticed when it disappeared from beside the old cigarette butts. (The fact that she tended to wobble into her bedroom after seven or eight beers didn't help her perceptiveness any.) Sophie had herself a ring and, to show her complete contempt for all that was natural in holy matrimony, wore it on the big toe of her right foot. She limped, but she was loved by the Dark Lord, wherever he was.

Whatever money she could scrape together eventually found its way into the cash register at "Chock Full Of Ghoulies." In no time at all, Sophie's bedroom was a museum of the occult. A genuine crystal ball sat on her night table next to her clock radio, into which she would endeavor to see the blackness in the souls of her next-door neighbors. Mystic runes, printed on blocks of wood and suspended on wire, hung from her bedroom ceiling in a pattern that she was certain would attract demons to her bedside. Each night, she studied a book of dark lore and decided that the devil's first name was Aleister, after that bald English guy who was on the covers of all the books in the occult store. She burned incense that made her sneeze, but that was alright because she knew her soul was traveling to her dark husband with each one. Black candle wax covered every horizontal surface. She bought an old record player at a yard sale for five dollars and played Led Zeppelin's untitled album at 78 rpms. Then she spun the album backwards very very quickly and thought she heard an inspiring phrase that she repeated over and over again as she drifted off to sleep.

Nothing happened.

Plays hard to get, she thought.

As the months wore on, her zeal began to diminish. She found herself dipping her fingers accidentally into hot wax as she reached for her hairbrush. Her nose was turning red and chapped from the hankies. The wedding ring produced a monster blister on her foot. She bumped her head on the suspended mystic runes. The Zeppelin album became scratched up beyond use and was thrown away. The crystal ball just sat on the edge of her table and didn't peek into the secret caverns of anyone or anything.

To anyone who cared to take any notice of her, Sophie had taken on the guise of a lapsed Satanist. She donned her usual attire, kept a bag of snuff on her at all times to periodically expel her soul, and wondered if it were seemly that a bride of Satan should be a virgin. It didn't seem acceptable to her own sense of logic, but she wasn't sure what could be done to remedy the situation. She told herself that she was saving herself for Aleister and tried not to let the reasons why she made that decision bother her.

And so it was when, on September 17, 2000, Sophie was finally rewarded for her persistence.

She'd been sitting on her bed, reading through an edition of "When The *BEAST* Comes A-Callin" by "Black" Peter Medway and listening to Marilyn Manson (backwards - something that she'd worked out on a friend's computer) when she decided it was time to expel a little more of her soul. She reached over to her handy pouch and produced a small wad of the magic tobacco. Seven months of practice had taught her that a little went a long way.

She absently lifted her fingers to her nostril and sniffed. The powder immediately went to work. As Sophie's eyes squinted in anticipation, her watery vision caught sight of a green glow next to her.

What the Hell was that?

A soft green veil floated against her closed eyelids. She felt heat on the side of her face.

Open your fuckin' eyes or your gonna miss it!

She sneezed mightily into the air and didn't even bother to sniff back the excess before her eyes sprang open and she turned towards the green light.

It was coming from the crystal ball.

The "Chock Full Of Ghoulies" special at $29.99 was glowing. It filled Sophie's eyes with a warmth she'd never felt before.

Sophie stared and tried to break through the light. The glow grew brighter and Sophie suddenly jumped up and quickly pulled down the window shades while barely taking her eyes from the crystal ball. This glow, this light, this brilliance, belonged to her and her alone and no one passing by was going to get a gander at it if she could help it.

Within the center of the light, deep within the ball, Sophie saw something move.

She peered deeper into the crystal. Tears began falling from her eyes as the green light pierced into her pupils.

I don't care! I don't care if I go blind and have to beg on the streets for the rest of my life! I'm gonna see what it has to show me! I'm coming, Master! Just tell me what you want! Tell me what you want! TELL ME WHAT YOU WANT!

She saw a room… a wall in some kind of public place. The vision was moving past small tables and getting closer to the wall.

Closer to a painting on the wall, a black and white rendition of a willow tree with branches blowing in a gale.

She fought against blinking, afraid to miss anything.

The painting was whipped aside and behind it was a hole.

A deep black hole in the wall.

...into the deep... the color is black...

And before she could gulp in surprise, the vision entered the hole. Did it fall or jump into it of its own accord? Sophie only knew that the eyes through which she was looking were falling deeper at an alarming rate. She could almost feel her hair blowing back at the force of the fall.

What's that? At the end. Something in the light at the end. What is it?

And with the suddenness of lightning striking a telephone poll, the glowing died. It didn't fade away or dim. One minute it was shining as bright as a house on fire, the next it was pitch black.

Sophie sat on her bed in the dark. A green haze floated in front of her eyes, leftover from the luminance of only a minute before. Once her eyes readjusted and they saw only the blackness of the dark room around her, Sophie seized the crystal ball from the velvet pad where it rested and shook it furiously.

"Goddammit, you cheap piece of shit! You think you can get away with that? What the Hell was that? You can't leave me like this!"

There was pounding on her door and a shaky voice from the other side that swallowed a belch.

"What's going on in there?" her mother shouted. Sophie could almost smell the scotch waft through the door.

"Shutup, Alkie!" she shouted back.

Her mother murmured something on the other side of the door, something that contained the words "kids," "respect," and "douchebag," before Sophie heard the footsteps staggering back to her own bedroom.

Although the shades were drawn, the window behind them was still open. The night made no sound. No cars drove by. No kids yammered about not wanting to take a bath. The crickets had evidently called it a night and turned in early. Sophie felt as if she was the only thing stirring on earth at that moment.

She knew where that painting was.

Such was her excitement that she didn't think about putting on her boots. Sophie ran out of the house with her torn slippers shielding her feet from the pavement. By the time she ran the sixteen blocks (actually lumbering along the last eleven of them, hoping she'd get there before her heart exploded), she'd lost one slipper somewhere along the way.

Within about twenty minutes, Sophie found herself in front of the Memorial Café, out of breath and ready to pass out. One glance from half a block away confirmed that her trip had been a waste of time and energy. The windows were dark, not the subdued dark caused by the low wattage bulbs but "Fuck-Off-We're-Closed" dark.

Sophie staggered the last half block up to the windows of the café and pressed her face against the glass. Inside all was quiet. Nothing seemed to be out of place, at least as far as the streetlamp behind her allowed her to see. Tables. Chairs. Counter. It was all there.

Including the painting of the Willow tree. Despite the darkness, she could just make it out on the opposite wall, hanging there like it always did.

She peered deeper through the window, hoping to somehow see

beyond the painting.

Fuck! Did it just move?

"Hey, young lady!"

Sophie turned to see a cop standing behind her. He was looking her up and down and had decided to focus on her feet. Sophie herself looked down and noticed for the first time that she'd lost one of her slippers. Her toes curled slightly under the cop's scrutiny.

"You're out kinda' late, ain't ya'," he asked, trying to tell at a glance what her story was.

"I only live on the next block over."

The cop looked up at the dark windows of the cafe.

"The place is closed. Ain't nothin' happening here."

"Yeah, I know." Sophie was surprised to find her mouth conjuring up words without any help from her brain. "I was here today and left my notebook in there. I gotta' test tomorrow and I was hoping to get it before they closed, but..."

"Too bad," the cop said. He kept looking at the windows.

Sophie kept going. "That's why I didn't bother to put any shoes on. I only live over there and I didn't expect that I'd be out for too long."

Shut your mouth. Only guilty people talk in airtight alibis.

But the cop wasn't listening. His focus was centered on the dark windows of the cafe. His eyes were lost in confusion and then fell into a glassy blankness.

Something's talking to him. I'm not crazy. There's something in there.

"So I'm free to go," she said.

The cop was silent for another moment and then blinked. His voice came back, but the forcefulness, the ring of authority that every policeman develops during his years in service, was completely gone.

"Move along."

The cop started to drift off in the opposite direction from which Sophie had come. He didn't look back at the café, but he didn't look forward either. His head was bent down, as if lost in thought. Sophie guessed that once he got far enough away, he'd find himself walking his beat again without any memory of her or whatever it was he'd heard at the Memorial Café.

I'll bet he requests a change of duty tomorrow, she thought and started the long walk home, limping most of the way. She would never know that the cop would instead abandon his beat, find his way back home, and slice himself straight up the middle of his stomach with a steak knife. Only his breastplate kept him from making it all the way up to his throat before the last of his strength ebbed.

Although Sophie walked back the same route that she came, she did not find her slipper. When she got home, her foot was bleeding. She bathed her feet and got ready for bed, taking care to place the crystal ball in her underwear drawer.

No more visions tonight, she thought as she sank into her pillow.

As she drifted off to sleep, she knew that she'd be going back to the café soon. There was something there that she just had to see.

In her dreams, Satan came to her and placed his furry claw inside her. He looked just like Ashton Kutcher.

Only God's To Give

(1995)
Rev. Jacob Grimsworthy

Hide from me... hide... I'm coming for you...

Edward lay on his stomach, on the roof of his new home (an apartment complex called the "Littleford Luxury Apartments" that boasted a misleading adjective in its name), and peeped through a pair of binoculars. His target, slightly under four and a half feet tall and dressed in a pink slicker to protect her from the light rain, was holding hands with her mother as they quickly crossed from the car to the protection of their own apartment complex across the street. He didn't know her name, the phrase "Pink Kid" went through his mind whenever he thought of her, and that was exactly the way he wanted it. Not that knowing her name would've made what he would eventually do any more difficult; those sort of second thoughts were reserved for those who had a conscience to bother them. And Edward, thankfully free of such constraints, felt that the air tasted sweeter and lighter when divorced from such piddling emotions. A fragment of memory still existed from when he could feel sorrow and pity, but they were like childhood memories, consigned to the old days of yesteryear when one believed that nothing bad – nothing *really* bad – could happen.

Bad things happen, little one. Things that you couldn't possibly dream of in your pink little imagination...

Still, the time wasn't quite right; five and a half weeks of surveillance had told him as much. The pink kid was supervised (...*guarded*...) quite well, even for the child of a family with no money or power. Her parents apparently loved the little shit and seemingly knew that dangerous forces could strike at them at any moment with no provocation whatsoever.

Good, thoughtful, protective parents... don't think for a minute that you can stop me...

In fact, not only was the challenge better with the more protective parents, but their grief dug into them deeper. He'd seen it many times on the evening news in the aftermath of his strikes: the frozen looks of shock that something as horrific as this could have possibly touched their happy little lives, the fleeting hopes that somewhere their sweet baby might be alive and might yet still come home, the fear in their eyes of the truth that they refused to acknowledge. All of this and more would be the fault of the man currently being lightly pelted by soft rain as he studied his prey through binoculars.

I've found a chink in your family's armor. Thursday from 11:30 to 12:15... the same every week for five weeks. Forty-five minutes... of which I need only one...

The pink kid and her mother turned a corner and went beyond Edward's sight, but he had already seen enough. He removed the binoculars and blinked in the grey, wet day, smiling and stretching his neck as the drizzle ran into his collar. In his old life, he'd found such a feeling discomforting but now, it was only experience: sensation to be felt and discarded.

As was everything else in life... feel it, experience it, digest it, expel it and move on.

He stood up, stretched his back and made his way to the ladder that had led him up to his perch. As he made his way, rung by rung, to the ground, the same idea passed through his mind over and over again:

...*today is Wednesday.... today is Wednesday... today is Wednesday...*

* * *

Edward never fully remembered his dreams; all he could remember as he felt himself waking up on that Thursday morning was that he'd been enjoying it immensely, which meant it must have had something to do with a young, terrified voice screaming out for mercy. But whatever it was that had allowed him to awake fully erect sped away when he opened his eyes and saw the man standing over his bed. Even in the haze of half-sleep, Edward recognized him immediately: the sad eyes, the rumpled blonde hair, the ruddy paunchy skin, all of it was the last thing he'd seen two years before when – still being human – he'd fallen unconscious. And those same features had greeted him after his soul-changing sleep, when he'd awoken to the sight of the concerned face repeating his name. And that was the first time that he'd realized that he'd been changed, that the worried face hanging over him meant nothing to him anymore. He'd smirked at the kind face and, when satisfied at the confusion that spread across it, had spat into it.

Edward's mouth was too dry for a repeat performance and so he simply smiled and croaked, "Hi, Henry."

"Hi, Ed," Henry replied. Edward's eyes trailed down to the coffee mug that his brother was holding. "I made you some coffee. Would you like some?"

Edward snorted. "You must think I'm a complete idiot."

"No, I... I just thought that you might..."

"... that I might just drink from a cup that you've had your hands on? Did you think that I would fall for that, or that I might even *welcome* it?"

"Ed, I..."

"You first!"

Henry looked down at the mug and started to lift it up to his lips. He faltered and realized that Edward, watching his every move, had just gotten all the proof he needed as to what was in the mug. Shaking his head, he put the mug on an end table. Edward had already risen into a sitting position by the time he'd turned back.

"And to think," Edward said as he flung the covers aside, not caring that he'd been sleeping in the nude, "you took an oath to preserve life. What must be going on in that head of yours'." He stood up, a full two inches taller than his older brother, and didn't flinch as Henry looked away to avoid the sight of his genitalia. Edward couldn't help but smile. "Come on, Henry. You're a doctor; you've seen naked men before. You can't blame me that I'm a bit excited this morning."

He laughed and brushed past Henry towards the bedroom door. Henry swallowed before calling out to him.

"And what are you so excited about? Planning something?"

"Planning an extra big breakfast," Edward called back. "You want me to make you one?"

Henry gritted his teeth and felt an urge to scrunch into a tight ball and wish with all his might that he was somewhere a million miles away. Instead, he tipped the mug of poison that he'd planned to serve to his brother over so that the hot muck settled into the carpet.

"Please don't take this the wrong way," Henry said as he left the bedroom and went to join his brother in the kitchen, "but why should I accept the hospitality of a man who wouldn't even take a sip of the coffee that I made for him?"

Edward let out a loud laugh that froze his brother in his steps; it was a sound that he'd never heard in Edward's first thirty-six years of life – all of his life as far as Henry was concerned. The last two years were...

Oh God, what have I done?

"Hospitality?" Edward's barking laughter nearly drowned out the word. "I don't remember inviting you here. Not that you were forbidden, of course; I seem to recall that I make you uncomfortable so I didn't think you'd accept an invitation to hang out."

Edward, still naked, had made it to the kitchen and was reaching for a large frying pan. He let the echo in his voice die and waited for Henry to respond, but there was none. All he could hear was the sound of his closet door opening.

"What are you doing in there?" he called out. Almost immediately, Henry stomped quickly out of the bedroom with a robe clasped in his hands.

"For God's sake, will you please put something on?" His voice shook as he thrust the robe out. Edward laughed and shook his head as if to say, "Same ol' Hen." He took the robe and wrapped it around his shoulders, but neglected to close it. Henry kept his eyes fixed on the ceiling.

"Aren't you going to close it?"

"It's hot in here."

"Edward…"

"I said, 'No.' Now stop crowding me."

Henry was surprised that he found himself nearly smiling at the whole situation. "Don't you have any…"

"No. You know that. If it bothers you, turn your back."

"Yeah, like I'd be stupid enough to turn my back on…"

"Oh, get the fuck out of here: you're in my way!"

Henry stepped back from the stove and retreated out to the dining table, never turning away from his brother. After sitting down, he took a moment to take in his surroundings: there was nothing on the walls and an opened box still held an assortment of unpacked kitchen implements.

"Nice little shithole you have here," he said.

"Can't complain," Edward said absently. He seemed totally absorbed in fixing his breakfast, whistling as he fetched the eggs and bacon from the refrigerator, not seeming to care that his guest had tried to poison him not ten minutes before. "You sure I can't tempt you?"

"That's a funny word," said Henry, "Tempt: to entice someone to do something that is thought to be immoral, used extensively in the Bible whenever the Devil wanted a good man to commit an abomination. But you've sidestepped all that, haven't you? No need to tempt Edward DeMarco: to tempt someone, you'd have to get him to jump over that hurdle known as 'Conscience.' And Edward DeMarco doesn't have to worry about that, does he? I mean, nothing like a conscience could have existed when he raped and murdered little Rachel Wrentham, could there?"

"I was referring to breakfast," Edward said, poking his head and penis around the doorway that separated them, "but talk about whatever you like, I'm listening."

Henry rubbed his eyes and felt like crying, but he held it back: this was not the time to be soft. "Why do you do these things?"

Edward cracked his eggs and was careful not to break the yolks. "How much time went by before you brought me back?"

Henry bit his lip. "You know how much…"

"How *MUCH?*" Edward never raised his gaze from the frying pan.

"Six and a half weeks," Henry admitted, rubbing his eyes even harder. "From April 19th to June the 3rd, if you want to be exact. You were dead exactly forty-six days."

The bacon was cooking rather nicely for a change so Edward shifted his attention to the eggs. "So I was preserved for forty-six days: my flesh, my heart, my brain… nothing atrophied. Nothing was lost.

My congratulations to you; you talked for years about preserving flesh and I never listened… I guess that'll teach me."

Henry felt like laying his head on the table in his disgust, but he knew it would be unwise to drop his guard. "Something *was* lost."

"And what was that?" He started humming as he flipped his eggs onto his plate.

"You. *You* never came back."

Edward giggled for a moment in the middle of his tune. He peeked around the doorway again. "Hey, so the experiment wasn't a 100% success. It's not like you're God or anything. Better luck next time." He disappeared back into the kitchen and laughed. "You certainly don't hear me complaining, do you?"

Edward fell back into the tune he was humming and the breakfast he was cooking. From the sound of it, Henry imagined he might even be doing a little dance in front of his stove. His eyes went back to the open box in which he could just make out a dish strainer.

Kitchen stuff… stuff like…

Henry had no idea how long Edward had been in the kitchen or how long it would be before he was finished cooking, but he knew that he wouldn't be in there forever. He had a narrow window within which to move and move he did, as quietly as he could, until he was crouching over the box. Beneath the strainer was an assortment of cups, plates and spoons that had never gotten put away. They would make a clatter unless he was careful.

His steady hand reached in and gently reached between strainer's rungs to the object he saw sticking up from amongst the spoons. Holding his breath, he pulled and came back with a small kitchen knife, only a few inches long, but it was serrated and had a good point at its tip.

So grateful was he that he'd managed to dislodge the knife without making any noise, that he nearly missed the absence of sizzling in the next room: Edward was nearly finished. Henry took three silent lunging steps from the box back to his chair and had just managed to hide the knife in his belt as his brother was emerging from the kitchen. In his hands were his plate and a small glass of orange juice. He also had a knife and fork and Henry was glad to see that Edward had chosen only a spreading knife to eat with. He was dismayed to see that Edward had still neglected to close his robe.

The brilliant doctor, who once exhausted every theory, resource and idea that he ever had just to experience the joy of seeing his dead brother's eyes open once more, felt decidedly ill as he fingered the knife handle and watched the thing that had stolen his brother's body eating his fried eggs.

"So," Edward said with his mouth full, "you say *I* didn't come back. Any theories?"

"What?" Henry was so fixated on what he intended to do that he hadn't heard a thing.

"Come on, Genius. You're so certain that I didn't come back, you must have some idea where the Edward you used to know and love went to; after all, matter can not be destroyed, can it?"

Just play along, he'll let his guard down… find the right moment and then…

"Uhhh... I... could only guess... something in the brain must have been damaged in the preservation process... something I didn't account for..."

Edward suddenly stopped eating and looked at Henry as if hit by an epiphany. "Maybe... maybe I went to Heaven!"

"What?"

"Well, you remember what I was like before, right? Pleasant, charming... wouldn't hurt a fly... went to church every Sunday... just the sort of guy who would get into Heaven after taking the long goodbye."

"What the Hell are you talking about?"

"It all makes sense now, don't you see? Here you are, restoring life to a dead body, just like Frankenstein, only better. I can walk, talk, think, and do anything that a normal person can do. But you couldn't give me a *soul* to work with, could you?"

Henry swallowed and felt sick. "Don't be stupid..."

"You gave me everything a doctor could, Henry. But you couldn't give me a soul. God's got it. Why, for all we know, I'm up there in the clouds at this very moment, playing a harp, flapping around, gettin' it on with Farah Fawcett..."

"Knock it off." Henry's fingers closed on the knife handle.

"You think Farah's up there? I hope I'm not settling for Mother Teresa or Maria Von Trapp. It almost makes it not worth it."

"Edward..."

Edward started laughing. "See? You're off the hook: you can't blame yourself for not giving me a soul. I guess you're just not God."

Henry's heart was beating so fast that he knew he would pass out in another minute if he didn't act fast. "I never said I was…"

"Let's put it to a test: turn my orange juice into a screwdriver and I'll consider worshiping…"

Henry lunged forward, the knife just coming out into the light, but Edward's iron grip clutched his wrist and arrested it in midair. Panicked, Henry realized he hadn't thought out his admittedly ill-prepared plan and was about to push himself away when he felt the dull edge of metal puncture his stomach. He was so surprised when he looked down that he dropped the knife: the spreading knife was sticking out of him.

He stabbed me with a butter knife! There's a butter knife sticking in my…

All he could see was the hilt sticking at a right angle out of his belly. There was remarkably little blood, something that Henry knew would change if he tried to pull the blunt weapon free. He tried to turn and felt the knife poking into his guts. As the throbbing in his stomach increased, his left arm went numb.

And then Edward was there in front of him with the kitchen knife in his hand.

"Impressive, right? And that was with a knife without an edge. Now this for example…"

The pain in his chest radiated to his back and shoulder and he prayed that his heart would stop before Edward took another step towards him.

Edward took another step towards him and held him by the throat.

"I'd say we'll see each other in Hell, but I'm already in Heaven, so what's the point."

It was all over seventy-two seconds later. Edward was a bit cross that his bacon had gone cold, but he finished his breakfast anyway, taking the occasional glance at what he had done.

The next day, the pink kid disappeared. Her parents searched and never gave up, but they never looked in the right place.

Or places. There were so many of them that eventually he forgot them all.

Except, of course, for the cooler that he always carried with him; everyday he'd take the time to gander at her little nose, packed in ice, sitting there at attention with all the other little noses.

Let's Get Dead

(1999)
Neil Ellison King

ey," she said, looking at me with eyes all googily and nearly rolled up completely into her head, "Let's get Dead."

Let's Get Dead [*letz - get - ded*] - Expression (circa 2050s) denoting the desire to partake in the consumption - through mouth, nose, vein, ears, tear ducts or rectum - of 35cc or more of byromanteen-mephilsulphate-C25 [see BMC] in 25ml or less of water. Other variations of same request include: ticket to Nevermore, apocalypse now, kill me, etc. - *Twenty-first century dictionary of American slang, 85th edition, Jason & Wagner Pub. 2086.*

Shit she was gorgeous. Her eyes, when I could see them, were the deepest blue in the world. Yeah, they were red now, practically all the way across, but I could remember how they punctured my buzz at the bar a few hours earlier.

Back there is Sully's place, she stuck her head between me and Curtis to order a Manhattan and, when Sully the bartender failed to notice her right off, she turned her head towards me. At first, my face was filled with blonde wavy hair that smelled of lavender, but then I saw her eyes and I was captured. At first, all she wanted was another drink. I knew that her being next to me was simply a quirk of chance. Another second and one of her friends would tap her on the shoulder and steal her away. I acted with all the verve that three vodka and limes can supply: I leaned over and gently kissed her jawline, making sure to nuzzle my nose up her cheek so that she would know that it was no accident.

She reacted immediately, rubbing her knee against my shin while never taking her eyes away from the bartender, ordering another Manhattan as if nothing was going on below the bartender's eyeline. I felt good and ready, wanting to kick Curtis off his barstool and let Blondie rest herself next to me. I inhaled deeper, hoping to get another lungful of her scent, but the bar was too full of other people that her perfume dissipated into the air.

She never looked at me the entire time that the bartender was making her drink; only when he placed it in front of her did she briefly glance my way to see what I was drinking. Then, quicker than a gymnast dismounting, she whipped her shoe off, a blue pump, and placed it on the bar.

"Give him another of what he's drinking," she said, "in *that*!"

She scooped her drink up and limped back to her friends. I reached over and stroked the sleek leather as the bartender shook my vodka with ice and poured it into her shoe, giving me a conspiratorial wink. He knew what was up and wished me luck.

Shoeing *n.* [*shoo-ing*] – Mid-twenty-first century flirtatious action consisting of a female offering her footwear to be used as imbibing receptacle of alcoholic beverage to potential sexual partner, male or female. Derived from early 20th century practice of drinking champagne from slipper of dancehall girls. Practice involves returning footwear after imbibing, with female's implied promise to wait for potential partner. In this practice, a female wearing both shoes denotes availability, while a barefoot female denotes over-familiar behavior. Females wearing open footwear (i.e. anything that can not be used consume alcohol from) are spoken for. *v.* to shoe. – to engage in shoeing. – *Ibid.*

You have to be careful in these types of places; you can't wait too long in finding your girl once she's shoed you. There's nothing worse than breaking your way through the crowd to your girl's table only to find some apekin holding her other shoe, looking to break your neck for the privilege of defending her non-existent honor. And this was just the type of place where apekins gathered by the dozens: howling until the dawn comes up with their blood full of Jizzmitine cocktails. I never touched the stuff myself, considering how quickly you had to get it down in order to experience the full effect (and why pay $46.73 a glass if you weren't going to go for the full effect), but any bartender who could mix an even halfway decent Jizzmitine could work magic on the old-fashioned cocktails and that's what I was in the mood for.

So there was no way I was gonna gulp it down, even if I hadn't paid for it (and even if I was drinking out of a shoe). But there was a time factor involved and that was in the forefront of my mind as I enjoyed my vodka and lime.

Apekin *n.* [*ayp-kn*] – 1. Derogatory expression denoting humans exhibiting the malady of genetic gorillism, a mutation characterized by large build, an intelligence quotient of less than 50 points and an excess of bodily hair (usually covering anywhere from 75% - 100% of the body). Condition is widely believed to be caused by the explosion of the Gorman-Lucus-

Tennant nuclear power plant in Birmingham, AL in 2026. 2.
Derogatory term for any large male. - *Ibid.*

Jizzmitine *n.* [*jiz-ma-teen*] - Alcoholic beverage distilled from the
nocturnal emissions of yaks, known for its immediate
intoxicating effects and earthy odor. - *Bottoms Up: Intoxicants
Of The Eastern World, Guildhall Pub. 2046.*

I met her at a table not far from where I had been sitting, laughing
with her friends. The beauties always hang together, don't they? All of
them were young, between twenty-three and thirty, sporting straight
white teeth in their laughing mouths and breasts that were just the right
size for a man to get his hands around without flopping over like a dead
jellyfish when it was finally time to get her on her back. And they were
all wearing just one shoe. So a whole group of them had gone out
looking for princes amongst the apekins and whiteguts that were always
hanging around, hoping against hope to be served a drink in a pump. I
reached into my jacket pocket and pulled out my hullospecs, something I
should have done back at the bar. A quick look through the purple lenses
would have told me everything I needed to know, but I'd had four vodka
and limes already and hadn't been thinking straight.

Whiteguts *n.* [wyte-gutz] - Derogatory expression for generally
unattractive males, assumed to find sexual solace through
excessive masturbation. Term derives from false belief that
excessive semen deposits, collecting on the stomach after
masturbation, turns a patch of the male stomach white from
over-saturation. *Twenty-first century dictionary of American
slang, 83ʰ edition, Jason & Wagner Pub. 2086.*

Hullospecs *n*. [hul-lO-spekz] – Plastic eye spectacles with tinted lenses allowing user to see through artificial coverings designed to increase the value of said item. Level of tints denoted by color (yellow, orange, red and purple) increase level of vision by user. The name is derived from the concept of penetrating hallucinatory surfaces and (with the introduction of the clothing-piercing purple lenses) the greeting "Hello" as many pairs were worn to penetrate the clothing of women in public. *Ibid.*

I didn't want to insult her, so I simply flashed the lenses in front of my eyes without actually putting them on, just for a second, but she turned towards me and caught me out anyway. She didn't seem to mind: she just laughed and put two thumb and forefinger circles to her eyes for the benefit of her friends, mimicking my specs. I was glad that she wasn't insulted because she checked out perfectly: no oranges in her bra, no girdle, no caps, no prosthetics, no squelgee. Even her thumbs were real, something I now *always* looked for. There's nothing worse than stepping on one of those rubber things laying on the floor in your bare feet while she's snoring and realizing that your next stop is the local clinic for a quick Fixer. Damn, but those girls with Glistenitis can fool you if you're not careful!

Squelgee n. [skwell-jee] – A flaccid penis. *Ibid*

Fixer n. [fix-r] – A booster antibiotic that guarded the human immune system against a variety of viruses. Although known to be effective against many ailments, fixers are common cure-alls against sexually transmitted diseases. The term "quick fixer" is an oft-used oxymoron as the procedure involves a long, drawn-out process that involves a pellet the size of a strawberry inserted rectally with the assistance of a sterile, remote-controlled robo-nurse. *Ibid*

Glistenitis n. [gliz-tin-**eye**-ts] – A contagious affliction, the main symptom of which is the melting of bodily extremities such as fingers, toes, outer-ears and, on male sufferers, genitalia. *Doctor, Can I Talk To You: A Guide To 21st Century STDs. Dr. Malcolm Savage. Heavyweight House Pub. 2067.*

The girls all hushed up, but were on the verge of laughing, as I approached their table with my girl's shoe. To her credit, she didn't make me put it on her for the benefit of her friends. She shook her blonde wavy hair out of her eyes and looked up at me, waiting for me to say the first words. The music was playing loud and I didn't relish the idea of shouting to be heard, but I knew the song would be ending in another twenty seconds, so I just took my time opening my mouth and instead drank in that gorgeous face.

She had one of those faces that you wanted to cup in one hand and hold up to your face so you could make her lips pout as they got closer to yours. There was nothing fake about her eyes either; I could tell that she'd been born with those piercing shadows around her eyes and hadn't needed to rely on a pencil to draw them in like most girls had to. Probably came from a long line of trampers, stretching all the way back to when Clinton was president if one was bothered enough to do the research (the third Clinton presidency, of course), and that was good: there wasn't going to be any fumbling or last minute case of nerves. I was looking at the best of my quest, the cream of the queens and the way she looked at me told me that she knew it.

Tramper n. [**tramp-r**] 1. An exotic dancer known for specializing
in a type of stomping dance reminiscent of ancient tribal
rhythms. The music for tramper dancing consists of a large
assortment of conga drums and a one-stringed instrument
known as a Gentar which plays upward note progressions as the
dancers reach fevered pitches. Trampers traditionally wear only
a cloth stretched across the nipples (known as a Bleedle), a flesh-
colored loincloth and a pair of Slooms (small cloth dancing
slippers). The action and ferocity of the movement is designed
to force the bleedle to tear away, exposing the breasts for the rest
of the dance. 2. Derogatory phrase to describe any physically
attractive woman. 3. Used comparatively to describe feats of
energy or activity, particularly in women. *i.e. She can run faster
than a tramper can stomp. Twenty-first century dictionary of
American slang, 85*[th] *edition, Jason & Wagner Pub. 2086.*

The song ended and, in that brief respite, I said, "What's your
name?"

"Miranda. Yours?"

"Dwayne." It wasn't, of course, but I suspected that I'd been lied
to first, so what the hell. It was all part of the ritual. Later, if she really
liked me, she'd sheepishly admit that her name was Doris or Gert or
something, but all that remained to be seen. The next song was starting
up and there wasn't much more to be said, plus I caught sight of the
ugliest apekin I'd ever seen heading for the table with a red ankle boot in
his hand. The girls at the table "ooohhed" and laughed at their nutty
friend who was already sticking her foot out to catch his attention. I took
a look at the girl wearing the other red boot, nice-looking with a full
mane of red hair and a pair of lips that could suck your brains out
through your squelgee if she felt so inclined. What the Hell was she
doing with that throwback? I began to suspect that maybe she was being

put up to it, that maybe all of them had something like that going, and I didn't want to have any part of a round of Dwimple, naturally shadowed eyes or not. Miranda seemed to read my mind and pulled me down so that her mouth was right against my ear.

"Natalie likes those kinds. Don't ask me why."

Since the level of sound was rising, what with her friends laughing and the next song now playing at full force, I had to talk right into her ear to be heard. "If you don't mind, I'd like to get out of here. I'd rather not get too close to those guys."

She didn't argue, or even say another word. Her friends were so taken by the monstrosity that Natalie had chosen to leave her boot with (the guy was still licking around inside it to get the last of whatever she'd bought him, probably a piss-warm pint of Pabst Blue Ribbon) that none of them noticed me help Miranda to her feet and make a quick exit.

> Dwimple n. [**dwim**-pl] – A game played traditionally by women in groups, consisting of teasing unattractive men, the goal of which is to see how long the male victim can be led to believe that the female's attention will lead to a sexual encounter. The game ends either when there is one player left who has a victim who has not guessed the nature of the situation or if, through a multitude of teasings, a victim is made to release an emission while fully clothed (preferably in a public place with one of the other players witnessing). *Ibid.*

I suppose if she'd had a pair of Hullospecs on her, she might've thought twice about me once she saw my car, but she didn't see anything amiss and I settled her into the passenger seat with the gentleness of a father putting his new-born daughter to sleep for the first time. She looked up at me and smiled. I leaned down and said, "Is there anywhere in particular you want to go to?"

She nodded and I was a bit disappointed; she knew where I wanted to go and she wasn't going to let me take her, at least not yet. Apparently a few drinks with her friends and a vodka-flavored shoe wasn't enough of an evening for her.

"Carfax Abbey."

Not bad. Sure, my bed was where X marked the spot on the only map I was concerned with, but if we had to go somewhere...

I wanted to ask her the obvious question, but I didn't want to insult her. Looking back, I realize now that she couldn't be insulted.

"Yes, I work there," she said, again reading my mind, or at least my ridiculous poker face.

"Isn't the show nearly over?"

"Not if you know the password."

Carfax Abbey pr. n. [kar-**fakz**, ab-bee] – 1. A term from literature: the old and crumbled building located next to Dr. Seward's lunatic asylum in London, UK, that is purchased and inhabited by Count Dracula in Abraham Stoker's gothic novel *Dracula. Ed.*

Jesus, didn't I say she was a tramper? And it wasn't enough that she was the prettiest girl at her table (or in Sully's), but I was surprised to find myself escorting the prettiest tramper in the entire place.

After ten, the cops made everybody leave the place and then parked their cars around the block before coming back for the good show. Everybody knew it, but very few knew the password, which wasn't a password at all but actually a dirty little secret of the police commissioner's that he desperately wanted to keep under wraps. When she knocked on the back door to the joint, the apekin on the other side let her in but put his big hand, mottled with smelly greasy hair, on my chest until I recited perfectly the phrase that Miranda had taught me on the way.

"Commissioner Doyle pays the morgue for children's livers because he likes to rub them all over his squelgee."

We got a great table, right down front where we weren't blocked by the apekins in uniform. The smell of all that sweaty hair was beginning to get to me, but there wasn't much I could do; door bouncers and the police force were the perfect jobs for apekins and, if you didn't like it, you went somewhere else other than Carfax Abbey after hours. I kept my nose in my vodka and lime (not as good as Sully's, but not bad either) and my fingers parked firmly around Miranda's thigh. She didn't mind; she didn't want any of the goons surrounding us getting any ideas and fingers tickling the inner thigh were all part of the ritual, letting everybody know that she was taken.

The show blasted me from here to next week. If I didn't know that Miranda and I were gonna end up in my bed later, I wouldn't have minded collecting a few shoes from that bunch. Usually it takes hours for the girls to warm up, but we were there at the right time and the congas started pounding as soon as the lights went up. One in particular stomped her feet so hard that I thought the stage was gonna collapse. She threw her head back like the best trampers do and her tits heaved against the bleedle. The cops whooped harder and some of them howled, letting their affliction get the better of them. I always hated that sound that apekins make when they get excited; it always sounded to me like a herd of elephants screaming from the shits. But as I said before, if you don't like it…

Well the trampers apparently did like it and they pounded even harder, especially the one closest to me with her head still reared back. Her slooms looked like they were about to split and then the crowd would have really howled because if there is one thing a bunch of apekins find more exciting than a bleedle going pop is a pair of naked feet pounding away on the floor. Got their priorities turned around, if you ask me; scientists have been trying for years to figure out how the apekin brain works and, if they have been rolling snake-eyes all these years, what chance did I have in the middle of a tramper show?

Must be the most secure job in the world: studying apekins. I suppose us tax-payers would be saved a lot of money if they all just ended their reports with the phrase "they're just fuckin' stupid," but there you go.

Anyway, the girl is stomping right in front of me, the room is boiling, the stench of mutant sweat is getting nauseating and this girl suddenly drops her head, takes one look at me and points at me without breaking step. Did she not see Miranda sitting next to me? Maybe she did and maybe not, but before I could do anything, I felt the muscles in Miranda's thigh tighten under my hand. Then I felt something cold being pressed against the back of my head. I knew exactly what it was and I wasn't disappointed to turn and see one of the servers standing there with a large drink in his hand, courtesy of whatever her name was up there on stage. They always have a few drinks in the cooler ready to go for when the trampers pick somebody.

What was I gonna do, turn it down? From where the server was standing, I even had to use the hand that I was formally using to fondle Miranda's leg. I turned to her and I could see she wasn't too happy, but she had this cool smoldering look instead of outright anger, as if she knew I was just a victim of circumstance. Her shoulders seemed to straighten up and, after a deep breath, she reached into her bag and pulled out an old tattered pair of slooms.

The cop sitting on her other side saw it and he panted his awful breath straight into our faces. He hooted and started pointing at Miranda as she kicked off her heels and slipped the slooms on her feet.

"Awww-haaaaaaa! She goin' up! Everybody; she goin' up! UP, UP, UP!"

I didn't try to stop her; truth be told, I was getting just as excited as the apekins around me (though I have a better sense of how to display my excitement in public). The rest of them were chanting *UP UP UP UP* as she leapt on stage in front of the other tramper, blocking her from my view. I think Miranda might have stomped down hard on the girl's toe, she seemed to break her rhythm for a moment, but trampers are trained to take that kind of punishment. Miranda squatted down so hard and fast that I thought she was gonna flip over and land on the back of her neck, but she sprang up again just as fast and started stomping like nothing that anybody had ever seen before. She didn't need to warm up or anything; she went from sitting to stomping and was keeping time with the rest of them.

True, she wasn't wearing a bleedle, just the nice dress that she had chosen for her evening out, but nobody in the club seemed to mind. I was so enthralled with how hard Miranda was moving up there (and amused to see Miranda take another stomp – this time there was no question – on the other girl's toes) that I nearly forgot my drink. I stuck my nose in it and sniffed (partly to rid myself of the smell of those damned cops) and couldn't believe it. A sip confirmed it: that pretty young tramper on stage (who was going to wake up with some ugly bruises on her feet the next morning) had bought me a Jizzmitine cocktail, a peach one if I wasn't mistaken.

Jesus Christ. A working girl had just paid for a fucking expensive drink and I was just sitting there letting my body heat warm it up. How the Hell was I going to tell her that she'd bought it for nothing; there was no way I was going to let Miranda go home with any of the apekins in the joint, and that's just what would happen if I chose the other girl. Hell, Miranda would be lucky to get off the stage as it was with all the excitement pulsing through the joint, bouncers or no bouncers.

But I wasn't going to waste that drink either. As it was, I would be lucky to get even half of the full effect considering how long I'd waited. I gulped down the first swallow.

Man, it was like an icicle shooting up my spine and exploding in my head. Ice crystals poking through my pours. The world turning blue around me. Mice running up and down my back with their little feet. Crying fire. A guy could get addicted to this. I steadied myself for another swallow.

And that's when the cop behind me, excited all out of his mind at the sight of Miranda stomping in front of him, pushed against me and the rest of the drink spilled on my pants.

The second I realized what had happened, the blue turned red, the ice in my head turned to steam, and I turned and smashed the glass into the cop's head. Not the smartest thing to do, I admit, but nowhere near as dumb as shouting, "You stupid fucking apekin! Buy me another fucking drink and I mean NOW!"

It's difficult to remember what happened next; I do remember realizing from the looks on the bouncers that they weren't going to be on my side just when a hand from up onstage grabbed me. Miranda couldn't pull me all the way up, so I scrambled up on stage as the whole place exploded in rage (and if there's one thing worse than the smell of a horny apekin, it's a raging one). I was still too drunk to know what was going on; Jizzmitine is so powerful that even a twelve-bell alarm like the one I was in the middle of won't sober you up much. I just let the hand gripping my shirt lead me to wherever it wanted me to go. I didn't get away clean: hairy arms pummeled me as I ran and I even got one good gut punch that nearly took me out for good, but the Jizzmitine cushioned it a bit, made it seem as if it was part of someone else's pain instead of mine. I knew I'd have to feel it full force when I sobered, but that was for later. Now was for moving.

I don't remember going through a door or anything, but suddenly we were outside and everything turned blue again. I was running fast now and didn't slow down until I heard Miranda's voice.

"We got away! Stop! I can't run anymore!"

I ran a few more steps and then let myself hit a wall so that I could give the poor girl a rest. My head was still pounding from the Jizzmitine and the pain in my guts was starting to become real again. I leaned over, feeling the wave of pain radiate from my stomach, and Miranda finally let go of my shirt. Even in the darkness, I could see that she was still wearing her ragged slooms; she'd had to leave her heels behind in the rush.

"Can you see any of them behind us?" I asked, panting. I didn't want to look behind me, afraid that my face would be recognized. She took a moment to grasp her left foot and rub it before answering, her smile never leaving her face.

"Don't worry. I can't hear anything. We got away. You wanna…"

She hesitated and her eyes grew wide. I can't say I ever saw her looking sexier that night than at that very moment.

"What?"

"You know."

Now it was my turn for my eyes to open. I could no longer feel the effect of the jizzmitine.

"You got some BMC?"

She didn't have to answer. It was a stupid question anyway.

"I live around the corner."

BMC [or Byromanteen-Mephilsulphate-C25] n. [Beye-ro-man-teen Me-fil-sul-fayt see-25] – A chemical compound created by Professor Miles Benteen in 2021, originally while experimenting on certain South American compounds in an effort to produce a hangover cure. The act of dissolving the crystals in water

produces the "Dead Effect": paralysis, muteness, slowing of
respiratory and cardio-vascular system while heightening sensory
experience. The effects of the Dead Effect are dependent on
the manner in which the compound is introduced into the
system. After the imprisonment of Professor Benteen in 2022
for the accidental living burial of a volunteer whom Benteen
assumed was deceased, the compound was made illegal to be
owned or administered anywhere other than a doctor's office.
The compound was made altogether illegal in 2061 following the
Premature Burial Scandal of 2059. *Ed.*

Her entire place was lined with tumbling mats. I guessed that
made sense; a tramper had to keep in shape without annoying the people
downstairs. And I just wanted to melt into it all as I walked in. Here I
was, still wobbling from the aftereffects of the jizzmitine and ready for
the two best feelings that Buddah had ever invented: fucking and BMC.
The mats were tricky to walk on and, after a few steps, I just let my legs
go to jelly and the mats rose to envelope me.

Oh, what a ceiling: white, pure white. Cream was dripping down
in front of my eyes.

And then she was leaning over me. The look on her face told me
that she had tried just the tiniest bit of it to make sure it was the real stuff.

"Hey," she said, looking at me with eyes all googily and nearly
rolled up completely into her head, "Let's get Dead."

"Let's indeed," I said, ready and waiting to see how she would
give it to me.

She poured it on my eyes, Saint Mary Save us! Good Christ
Almighty with a squelgee to match: right in my EYES!

drip drip drip drip drip drip drip drip drip... right into me...

I can see into you.

Right into you.

I can see the tumor at the base of your left occipital that will kill you in twelve years.

I can see the dust in your mucus membranes that will make you sneeze in two minutes.

I can see the traces of the baby you aborted five weeks ago.

I can see them coming... the cars are approaching. They didn't turn the sirens on.

I can see them talking... splitting up and sneaking up on us.

I can't move. I'm dead.

I can see you just about to get dead yourself... you've got the dropper poised above your eyes.

Is that beating I hear your heart or mine? Or is it the door bursting open?

And then there's hair... mangy mottled hair flailing from the arms and the faces of those who are suddenly there. I hear things.

"There he is.!"

"We've got him!"

"Apekins, huh?"

"Not so fast now, huh?"

"No! Stop! He's under! Please don't hurt him!" That was you. That's when I fell in love with you. You tried to save me.

I wanted to jump up and protect you from them, but I couldn't. I couldn't move. You wanted me to move but I couldn't... I tried but I couldn't... I couldn't... I couldn't...

"Leave me alone!"

That's what I heard you say as they dragged you into the next room. You kept screaming over and over... and the cops kept on whooping... the way that apekins do... over and over...

I'm dead! I can't help you... I'm dead...

They're standing over me, grinning and drooling. All I can I feel is a sloom lying just beyond my fingers. Soft... so soft...

"He ain't gonna make it."

"Nahp."

"Too bad."

Oh God... what are you gonna do to me? I'm sorry for what I said... I didn't mean it... please leave me alone...

I saw one of those mangy hairy hands dip the eyedropper into the vial. Then he raised his claw over my eyes...

No...

The Premature Burial Scandal of 2059 – Name given to the series of illegal burials of living people suffering from the "Dead Effect" of Byromanteen-Mephilsulphate-C25. In August 2059, approximately 367 police officers throughout the United States were prosecuted for secretly funneling bodies of people who were temporarily paralyzed by the effects of Professor Benteen's compound to black market doctors who harvested the bodies for much-needed organs and buried the remains. It had also been discovered that certain perpetrators simply buried people (sometimes after forcefully administering the drug to the victim) to satisfy personal vendettas. Although defense attorneys argued that the accused officers could not be held responsible for their actions because of mental instability (most of the accused officers were sufferers of genetic gorillism), public outcry over the scandal led to the banning of Professor Benteen's compound in all its forms and a reassessment of the practice of hiring genetic gorillas in law enforcement. A total of 586 bodies were exhumed in the aftermath of the scandal, with investigators saying that they had uncovered "only a fraction of all the victims of this inhuman practice." *Ed.*

It's dark down here.

More: A Tale Of Capitulation

(2007)
Sinead Meldrew

She sleeps on knives. On nails. Her wrists and ankles suspended by hooks. It doesn't hurt her. Well, it does but it doesn't. You wouldn't understand.

When she stirs, there's a marvelous scratching along her back. It pierces her and she coos with delight.

This is how to live.

At eight o'clock in the morning, Roderick comes in, never late and never early. You can set your watch by him. Some mornings, she can hear him counting the seconds quietly on the other side of the door to make sure he enters just at the right time. Not too quietly, though; he isn't very bright and if he doesn't count at least partially out loud, he'll lose his place. And then he'll be late. And then he'll be punished.

Like last time. When dinner consisted of left-testicle stew.

Fifty-six… fifty-seven… fifty-eight… fifty-nine…

The door opens and Roderick is inside with his head bowed and his voice not creeping above a mumble. He isn't meant to look upon her, but he also just doesn't want to see what is there in front of him.

"Good Morning, Mistress," he mumbles.

No answer. That tends to be a good sign. If she were cross with him, she'd let him know immediately. Instead, a few seconds pass while she takes in a deep breath and lets it out with a contented whistle in her throat. Still suspended by the chains, a three-foot sharpened spike rests in the curve of her spine, just barely poking the skin.

"Mmmmmmm. Good Morning, Roderick. Hoist me."

Roderick bows and, making sure his hands have stopped shaking, takes hold of the rusty crank installed in the wall beside the bed. It makes noise and her eyes grow wide at the sound, but that's her morning pick-me-up. Roderick puffs as his mistress's body raises up four or five inches higher, clear of the spikes below her but rising precariously close to the spikes affixed to the ceiling. But the needles are what bothers him the most, even after all these years. They hang so low, so sharp, so poised to be buried into the mistress's flesh. Not that she would mind, of course. To her, the sting of the odd needle or spike is another moment of bliss, a confirmation that blood still flows through a beating heart, and tears will fall because what more can you ask of life than to feel the flow of blood passing through you every second of every day? No matter what gives you that feeling, can it be bad?

She's hanging from hooks, attached to chains, and the flesh through which the hooks have penetrated is throbbing.

"I'm hungry."

"Yes Mistress."

He's left the plate outside the door, and he bends to fetch it. What can be said about what's lying there, waiting to be consumed: a broken bottle, smashed only a few moments before he'd climbed the stairs to wake her?

As he bends down to retrieve the plate, something inside him hitches. He hiccups and feels his stomach beginning to gurgle. Something slimy creeps up into his throat and he tries not to cough, for to cough means to vomit and to vomit means punishment.

"What's wrong?"

"Nothing, Mistress."

Some mornings, she would pursue it, wanting to hear him say it because even that is nectar to her. How can it not be? But this morning she just wants sustenance of the more immediate kind.

Roderick lifts up the tray and the sun coming through the window glints off the shards of glass. No piece is bigger than the pad of his thumb, except for the neck and base of the bottle which lay there only partially smashed. That's part of the regime too: she wants the big pieces there, just in case she's feeling a bit hungrier than usual.

"That looks good, Roderick." Her voice is quiet and filled with fetid breath. It's not easy to make yourself understood while hanging from chains. And besides, now is not for talking. That look has come over her, all wide-eyed and expectant. And her mouth has opened and her scarred tongue has lolled out, almost a beast with a mind of its own.

Roderick picks up the first shard and can't help but let his hand shake a bit as he brings it closer to the tongue, which practically scoops it out of his fingers and flips it down into her mouth. Her tongue folds in on it and then she starts chewing.

And smiling. And when she flashes that toothy grin, blood bubbles up from between her teeth.

And does Roderick watch all this? Yes, because that's part of what makes her happy. So he watches as she starts to cough and choke as the blood seeps into her throat. He watches as she turns her head and spits out the blood and coughs until her face turns red. And her chest heaves heavily and comes close to being pierced by the low-hanging spikes. And after it all, she laughs because it's funny in its own way, isn't it? Can't you see the funny side of all this, Roderick? She's not Superwoman or some kind of circus freak, is she? She's bleeding, she's feeling pain, she's killing herself, but she *loves* it, don't you see? I mean, that's got to make you laugh, right?

And she's making you watch. You gotta see the humor, can't you?

She finally catches her breath and turns her head up to look at him again. Her teeth are stained red and there is blood running down both sides of her face. When she speaks this time, her tongue is working past the fresh lesions, which she'll force him to sew up later.

"M-m-mmore!"

And so it goes. Roderick shoves piece after piece of jagged glass into the waiting and grasping mouth until he can't ignore the spinning of the room anymore. The tray shudders in his hand.

"M-mmmmmore, R-r-rrrodurrrrrik! Mmmmmmmorrrrrrrrrre!"

But instead of passing out, he finds himself waking up. Despite how horrible the nightmare was, he doesn't scream out; he's used to the nightmare. He's had it practically every night for years.

He looks over at the clock beside his bed and registers the time: 7:15. It's time to get up. There should be just enough time.

At two minutes to eight, he finds himself standing next to the closed bedroom door, counting the seconds. She doesn't like to be disturbed before eight. You could set your watch by him.

Fifty-six… fifty-seven… fifty-eight… fifty-nine…

He knocks.

"Rod, is that you?"

Who else could it be, he doesn't say. Who else would do this?

"Yes, Mom."

"Come in."

Rod enters just as his mother is attempting to raise herself into a sitting position on the bed, all three hundred and six pounds of her. The tortured springs groan in protest and Rod puts his tray down to help her. It isn't easy, the mattress has permanently settled into her normal sleeping position and the smell makes being as close to her as he has to be unbearable. But like every morning, they finally succeed.

"Thanks." Her voice is husky from labored breaths.

"We should get you a new mattress. I think the springs might be gone on this."

"Nah, why waste money."

"I'm surprised the springs aren't digging into you."

"It don't bother me. You got breakfast?"

Rod retrieves the tray, piled with a stack of pancakes and sausage patties, swimming in maple syrup. Her eyes gleam hungrily at the stack of food as he brings it closer. Her mouth opens even before he's had a chance to cut off the first bite.

Her bloated tongue lolls out and waits for the first taste, beckoning him.

Once the first mouthful is lovingly chewed and swallowed, she makes a contented groan. Sweat is breaking out on her forehead, the result of a heart working so hard to keep her alive.

"That's perfect, Rod. More."

Can't you see what's happening to you… what you're making me do?

"Remember when I used to feed you, Rod? Funny how things work out."

And it was funny, if you looked at it the right way.

The Button Pusher

(2010)
Delaine Paroczai

Night time again. At least he thought it was. And what I think, goes, he thought. That's the way it is and that's the way it'll stay. Power of life and death must mean something.

The man sat at his desk and pondered. That's my job, he thought. Pondering. Until the day the red light goes on.

He looked up above his workstation and regarded the light. He didn't stare. What was the point? It sat sticking out of the wall, a great glass bulge waiting to scream, to blast, to be free. The man looked at it and waited, knowing that today would not be the day. Neither tomorrow nor the next day. The light was silent and would remain silent for days to come, probably years. And with the years of silence so would he be silent. That was his job. Be silent. Keep under cover. Do the cool and chilly thing.

Until further notice.

When the time comes, you'll fulfill your function. You'll push a button.

People all over the world will know what you've done and what you were put on Earth for. Just sit tight and try not to think too much about what you're doing down here. We'll tell you what to do when the time is right. Keep quiet until then. Keep quiet. You'll make your noise when the time is right. Quite a noise indeed. What a noise. What a noise! What a...

The man, called Dave, also known as the Last God of Destruction, sat alone in the control room of his offices. This was the room that he, and only he, was allowed to work at. There were several other rooms branching off from this one. Not many, only the few that he needed so as not to feel too cramped.

He looked to his right and saw the steel, sliding door that led to his bedchambers. A good bedroom with a comfortable bed lay beyond that door. It was a steel room covered with movie posters. *The Exorcist, The Adventures Of Baron Munchausen, The Manchurian Candidate, Animal Crackers, El Topo, Ganja & Hess, The Last Waltz...* nearly every millimeter of shiny silver surface was covered. He'd fall asleep looking at them all and forget what his job was.

In his bedroom was a curtain over a doorway, leading into a bathroom. There were also two other sliding doors. They were set in the wall facing his bed and were the only surfaces in the room that were not covered by movie posters. Left and right. Howdy and Doody. Lennon and McCartney. The one on the left led to a small chamber where his refrigerator, stove and cupboards were. Each Thursday, he tried to play his music loud enough to drown out the sounds of the clumsy men who came through the kitchen's outer door to fill his cupboards and refrigerator with everything he wanted. When they were finished and had gone their way (they apparently knew how to open the outer door and escape; it never opened for him no matter what he tried) he'd have everything he needed for yet another week.

Every fourth Tuesday evening, a girl would be standing there.

A girl with a painted face and teased hair, teetering on painfully high shoes. A girl wearing thin, cheap clothes would provide living color and compete with the movie posters. More likely than not clutching herself and shivering from the chill in the air that he'd long since grown accustomed to. Sniffing, she'd look up and smile at him and he'd lead her to the bedroom where she'd do what she'd been brought to do.

Whatever he asked for.

And the next morning, he'd nudge her awake, push her out of the bed, force her to gather up her clothes and point her towards the sliding door on the right.

The one he'd never gone through.

He didn't know what lay beyond that door. He imagined a long corridor, but wasn't sure. Once, he'd peeked from beneath the covers and saw that month's girl immediately taken under each arm by two soldiers who were stationed (hidden?) on either side of the door. The door had swished shut so quickly that he'd seen nothing more, but he'd heard the clacks of the soldier's boots as they marched her down the hall. All sound receded and echoed down the corridor that he imagined was there.

He'd reached over, grabbed the remote control and pointed it at the stereo system with the ceiling-high speakers. Unfortunately, he'd been a little slow on the draw. He happened to catch just a taste of the gunshots echoing down the imagined corridor before the speakers exploded in music.

He'd laid there for two hours, letting the system randomly pick his music for him until he got up and went into the control room, where the buttons were, where the doors to the outside were but which would not open until quite a while after the buttons were pushed.

Each morning after a girl's visit, he would sit down tired and nauseous, trying to forget what probably happened to the girl and looked at each and every button in front of him, nine hundred and thirty-six in all.

Each button a missile.

Each button a destination.

Each button a million people dead.

Dave was under orders to wait until he was asked to fulfill his purpose. Until then, he would wait in his underground bunker and all his needs would be provided for.

* * *

One Tuesday, he opened the left-hand sliding door and found himself captivated by the woman standing awkwardly in his kitchen. She had dark brown hair that fell wavy around her shoulders. She wore a blue sweater that kept her warm down to just past her elbows and just above her navel, where the fabric ended. Her short skirt ended just above the knees, which trembled slightly out of both nervousness and the chill. Her toes, encased in low-heels, pointed inward, pigeon-like. She looked up, startled as the door slid open and Dave was struck by the wide, naked beauty of her lightly made-up eyes. She looked him up and down and looked even more confused.

"Problem?" he asked.

Her mouth opened hesitantly, trying to find words to speak.

"Excuse me," she finally said. "I... I don't know you, do I?"

"If you did, you wouldn't be here." He stepped aside and extended his arm into the chamber beyond, inviting her in.

The girl stood in his kitchen, not certain what to do. She looked beyond him, into the bedroom. The movie posters and the shaggy rug covered the antiseptic atmosphere. But still, the entire situation had raised warning sirens in the girl, too late to do her any good.

"I was expecting the Grand Executive."

"Is that what they told you?"

"No, not really. But with all this security, who else could it have been?"

Dave smiled. "Me, for a start."

The girl still held back. "They made me sign an oath of secrecy. It was sixty-five pages long. I tried to read it but..."

"But your eyes started hurting and all you wanted to do was get this job over and done with because time is money and it all looked pretty official anyway."

"Yeah, something like that."

She sniffled loudly and rubbed her nose. It was the chill of the room. Dave had detected it getting colder since he entered. His eyes darted briefly to the vents near the ceiling; the cold air seeping through them was almost visible. It was a subtle ploy on behalf of whoever had delivered the girl to get her into the bedroom, where the warm bed sheets were.

They're watching… or least listening. That shouldn't bother me at this stage of the game.

"It's cold in here, isn't it?" she asked, sniffling.

"It's warm where I'm standing."

The girl finally made up her mind and proceeded past him into the bedroom. Her step was cautious, as she never realized that her final decision had been made long before she'd arrived in his kitchen. He wasn't sure if her point of no return had come in whatever secret room they'd presented her with the oath she had to sign or when they'd picked her up on the street, but it had come long before this meeting and there was no turning back.

"Oh, this is much nicer," she said. The stuffiness had left her voice and she sighed in comfort. Dave saw her do as all the others did when comforted by the warm air; she tossed the jacket she'd been carrying onto the nearby chair and slipped her feet out of her shoes, scrunching them into the shaggy carpet.

Dave followed her and closed the door.

* * *

She was new at this.

It was something she did.

Everything had gone well at first. The kitchen door swished silently shut, blowing one last puff of chilly air into the bedroom, at 9:07.

At 9:12, her clothes were off.

At 9:13, his clothes were off.

At 9:14, they were under the sheets.

At 9:22, he was licking her left nipple.

At 9:27, she was rubbing her toes along his leg.

At 9:36, he came.

At 9:37, she giggled and rolled over, falling fast asleep a minute later. He simply laid next to her, staring up at the ceiling and replaying the entire thing in his mind.

It'd taken him a long time to reach 9:36, much longer than usual. Under normal circumstances, 9:36 would've happened by 9:24 at the latest. Something she did had put him off, had given him pause, had ruined the whole fucking thing.

Something she'd done at 9:23.

She hadn't meant to. He knew that. She was young, inexperienced, and it just slipped out.

Actually, it glided out on a warm whisper and drifted into his ear, a tinkling song of grace breaking through the sweating and groans.

"I love you."

She couldn't have meant it. He knew that. Young... inexperienced...

He looked over at her as she slept, breathing only the tiniest bit, silent, with a barely noticeable smile on her lips. He noticed how soft her hair looked for the first time as it splayed around her head on the pillow.

He rolled over and knew he'd be pretending to sleep all night, pretending for her in case she woke up and for himself to try to convince himself that nothing had changed.

I'll sleep straight through it all, he thought. The opening of the door...

…the boots down the corridor…

…the shots…

* * *

To his great shock, he did indeed drift off to sleep, but only after hours of lying in the dark. The greater shock came when he awoke the next morning and saw her, half-dressed and heading towards the right-hand door. His eyes opened lazily as her hand reached out to the large button next to it.

With a gasp, he shot up and was sitting straight up in bed.

"STOP!"

Somehow, in a room covered with plush rugs and movie posters, his voice rang. It was enough to stop her in her tracks. She turned to him.

"What?"

Good question, he thought. What now?

"Look, Ms.… uh… what is your name?"

She looked at him squarely. "They said I wasn't supposed to…"

"Look, who do you really think is running things around here: them? Trust me, the last thing they want to do is disappoint me."

The girl walked back to him and held her hand out.

"So, you're the one with the cash, are you?"

"What?"

"My three thousand dollars, I'll take it now."

Dave looked at her outstretched palm and felt small, the tiniest he'd felt in years. His power over life and death over the entire world wouldn't conjure up three thousand dollars in the next five seconds.

"That's what they promised you?"

"That's what I earned, Bud. You may be The Glorious And Imperial Poobah in your little room here, but you ain't the one with the three grand, which means you ain't the one I made the deal with. *They* got their rules, pages of them. I didn't read them all, but I did see the part that said I would forfeit my money if I deviated in anyway from the general orders: as much sex as you wanted, as little talk as possible, leave by the right-hand door by nine o'clock sharp and that's what I..."

She stopped suddenly, looked at her watch and gasped.

"Fuck! I'm two minutes over! See what you made me do! If you blow this for me..." She turned and started running for the door.

Dave was up out of the bed and would have beaten her to the door if his leg hadn't tangled in the blanket. He fell on his side with loud "ooof." She turned back for only a moment, scared but still concerned for a man who'd just nearly fallen on his face. The moment was all that Dave needed as he scrambled up and headed for her. The girl squeaked in surprise and slammed her hand against the button. A second later, the door swished open and two soldiers, stationed on either side of the door, reached inwards. Their bulky arms, encased in neatly pressed sleeves, grabbed for her and she jumped back - no longer certain which direction the greater danger now lay in. A strangled "wait" escaped from her throat. The large hand on her left got a strong hold of her sweater.

Dave was over to the girl before she could scream for help. But she screamed anyway as the hands grabbed at her and pulled her through the door. Dave plunged between them, grappling with the beefy arms that held her. The guards' movements stilled for a moment, knowing that the Last God of Destruction was currently pulling at their arms, and the guard on the right actually yelled in anticipation of the bolt of electricity that would shoot through him at this unthinkable moment of contact.

It was all Dave needed to wrest the girl from the guards' grasp and push her to the floor. In the same movement, he pivoted and slammed his hand against the button. The door swished shut, but not before the guard on the left fired a bullet past Dave's head that twanged and shattered on the wall over his bed, catching Tom Cruise in the *Eyes Wide Shut* poster right in the nose. The explosion of the shot nearly burst his ears; it even drowned out the girl's scream.

Dave stood with his hands flat against the door, breathing heavily. Behind him, the girl whimpered, trying to find the strength to ask him what had just happened. He couldn't talk to her, not just yet.

He felt a tapping at the door: low, hardly audible, frightened.

He placed his ear to the door and hissed: "Go away."

"We're sorry."

"We didn't know…"

"Just don't do anything."

Dave smiled as he tasted the worry, the downright terror, in those whispered voices.

What do they think I'll do? Do they think I'll…

He heard the girl scramble up and run to the sliding door she had come through the day before.

"You can't get out that way."

She stopped, her hand wavering before the button.

"It opened for you yesterday."

"That's my kitchen. It'll open, but the far door won't. Only they can open it and you've already seen how anxious they are to talk to you."

The girl backed away from both the door and him. She fell back against the far wall, looking not at all at home in this homey room.

She looked to the third door.

"Are there any guards in there?"

"That's where the buttons are."

She decided to save the obvious question for later... if there was one.

"Can I get out through that way?"

Dave bit his lip.

"There is one door leading to the outside world, but it's locked. It won't open until I press a button."

"A button?" the girl asked.

"Yeah." Dave trudged over to the bed and sat down.

The girl looked at him expectantly. "So why don't you..."

"And even then it would take thirty years for it to open."

The girl slid down the wall until she was sitting on the floor, her face a mask of shock. Dave only looked at her plainly.

"So what's your name?" he asked.

* * *

Her name was Tracy. She was twenty-five. She had an apartment on the lower west side. She had a mother in Spokane that she didn't see very often. She had all the Pink Floyd albums up to "Wish You Were Here." She had a dog named Spunky. She had a mole on her right hip. She had back pain from time to time. She had ticklish feet.

She had a thing about guys touching her ears. She had grave misgivings about what she'd gotten herself into.

Dave showed her all around. It took him all of seven minutes, but he did it anyway.

"This is mission control," he said, leading her into the control room, the metallic doors going *swish* behind her and making her even more anxious. "This is where it all happens."

He snickered.

"Or, at least, where it will all happen eventually."

Tracy didn't like the sound of that at all.

"Eventually?"

"Sure. Haven't you been watching the news? Every day it gets worse. Every day, they get closer to giving me a call." Dave leaned closer to his control panel, fixing his attention at the silent red bulb above all the buttons.

Tracy stepped back slightly. She heard Dave sigh long and longingly.

"That bulb could be a dud," he said.

"What?"

"Well, it's possible. I've never seen it light up. There's no way to test it." He turned to her. "Wouldn't that be something? People may have been waiting for years for everything to fly to smithereens and here I am, waiting for a dead light to go on…"

"Years?" Tracy's mouth had gone dry and only one word came out.

"Well, twelve years anyway. Before then, who knows?"

Dave continued to stare at the dark bulb. Tracy stared at the room around her.

The chamber was a sharp contrast from the sloppy hominess of Dave's bedroom. The walls and floor were metal, not clean and gleaming, but dull with age and neglect of proper care from a cleaning service. The room was empty except for the immense control panel, littered with buttons, the twenty-seven television screens mounted on the wall in front of it (all switched to various news stations around the world - all silent and spouting their propaganda via closed captioning), and the dark, red bulb above it all. There were two doors, besides the one she'd come through, on the far walls.

"Is that the one that won't open for another thirty years?" She pointed to the one opposite the control panel.

Dave glanced at it and grunted. She looked past Dave to the other door.

"And that one?"

"Non-perishable rations," he said, still gazing at the light. "That one opens as soon as I press one of these buttons. They don't want anything getting in the way of me doing my job, so they provide me with everything: Choice-cut meals while they're still here, rations when they're gone, no chance of being infected myself, no one to miss on the outside world..."

His voice died down and Tracy saw him drop his gaze from the lamp. His face clouded with apprehension.

Tracy shivered. "I want to leave."

Dave sat down in his swivel chair and swung towards her. "Are you crazy?" he asked. "Didn't you see what they tried to do to you when you tried to leave last time? Can't you see that you're a security risk? Do you think that they'd want the story of the man in the underground chamber with all the buttons to start floating around the streets?"

Tracy looked at the wall and saw herself walking the streets again with Spunky, going to see her friend Shirley, hanging at the local bookstore, taking in a movie or sitting beneath a tree in the park with a book; the book she'd left by her bedside two nights before and had been hoping to get back to once this job was finished.

The book she'd never get back to.

Dave slowly stood up and went to her, awkwardly putting his arm around her shoulder. She thought about moving away from him, but another realization came to her too quickly for her to resist.

He was a nice guy.

He had saved her life.

And he was her only friend. Her shoulders relaxed beneath his arm.

"They give me food. Good stuff. Anything that I want."

Tracy breathed deeply, her breath hitching as she thought about what lay before her.

"Not just food, either. I mean *anything* that I want is a written request away. What do you want?"

Tracy looked up at him squarely, her brows set.

"Don Quixote."

* * *

It was there, on the kitchen table, an hour later, along with the groceries that Dave had typed into his wish list. His wish list - as he called it - was nothing more than an email program designed to transmit to his handlers and no one else. That day's list was short, though elaborate, and to the point.

```
Two (2) steaks (super-lean),
Spanish Rice,
Fresh Asparagus,
One (1) bottle of Pinot Noir - 1957,
One (1) quart of vanilla ice-cream,
One (1) copy of Don Quixote by Cervantes,
Zero (0) funny business… or else.


        You Know Who.
```

He heard them come and go behind the sealed kitchen door. He heard a beep within, the sign that the auto lock on the far door had activated. The green light above the door flashed on, telling him that the pressure-sensitive floor could not detect anyone's bodyweight treading on it. Still, he asked Tracy to step into the control room as a precaution. He knew it was needless but he felt better as he punched the control pad and the kitchen door slid open before him, revealing nothing more than the bag of groceries and the book sitting on the table.

"Tracy," he called out. "Coast's clear."

He heard Tracy approach. She was hesitant and peered around the doorway.

"I told you," he said, "everything is fine. They're not going to try anything. Just take your book and sit back a bit while I fix dinner."

He swiped the book off the table and tossed it to her in one move without so much as a "think fast" to warn her, but she caught it anyway.

"Mind if I use your bed?"

"Make yourself comfortable," he said and turned his attention to the shopping bag. She stopped, considering for a moment, and turned back.

"I want a cat."

Dave continued rooting through the bag, finding the ice-cream and handling it gingerly as the cold tub stung his fingertips.

"What kind of cat?"

"Something with a lot of fur that won't mind not going out very often."

"Okay."

Tracy smiled and left. Dave quickly deposited the ice-cream in the freezer and returned to the task he'd set himself.

An hour later, he was just putting the finishing touches on the two plates he'd set. The steaks were perfectly broiled. He'd found some onions and mushrooms to fry up. The asparagus was steamed and the rice fluffy, the Spanish seasonings leaving a faint spicy aroma.

All I need is a bit of parsley on the side that we can push around with our forks and ignore.

"Tracy," he called out. "It's ready!" He picked up a corkscrew and applied it to the bottle. He'd never been good about opening wine without breaking the cork into bits. So intense was he with trying to spill as little of the cork into the wine as possible that he didn't notice that Tracy hadn't answered him until the wine was in the glasses.

"Tracy?"

There's no other way they can get in... is there?

He crept to the door and looked into the bedroom.

Tracy was lying on the bed, her face a white mask of misery.

Dave rushed in and grabbed her hand, knowing that she was still alive before he touched her, but grateful to feel her blood flowing just the same.

"Tracy, what is it?"

He saw her other hand lying on her lap. A scrap of paper, folded several times to fit within the book's pages, was clutched in her fingers. *Don Quixote*, the unwitting messenger of the note, lay forgotten next to her.

Dave picked up the note and read it silently.

```
Dear Ms. Baxter,
    I'm very sorry that my men frightened
you so this morning.  It was not their
intention to cause such a ruckus.  I
completely understand your unwillingness to
continue with the arrangement as we agreed.
If put in the same position, I would be where
you are now.
    However, I must stress that a contract
is a contract.  You have, through your own
choice and free will, entered into the
agreement and we expect you to follow through
on every detail as outlined during our last
```

meeting. You know as well as I do that the
agreement terminates the moment you step out of
the door indicated on the map that we showed
you earlier. My subordinates have informed me
that you have failed to do so. This may be a
simple error on your part and if so, we can
both forget this little setback. In fact,
because of the over-eagerness of my men this
morning, I'm perfectly willing to extend a
fifty percent bonus for your trouble.

However, I also know that our friend down
there is no lover of romantic literature. I
have the sneaking suspicion that you are
willingly staying on past the agreement. I
must warn you that this is an unconscionable
move on your part.

I don't know what our friend has told
you, but he is far from the independent warlord
that he fancies himself to be. It takes the
effort of thousands of people to keep him where
he is and it takes only one misaligned cog to
bring down the whole machinery. If he told you
that we can not get to you in that cozy little
bedroom, think again. We've spent too much
money on this project just to have it
jeopardized by you. The situation down there
must be brought back to the routine that we
have determined to be optimal for our friend to
do his job. That leaves no room for you.

```
        Leave the bedroom by the door we
    specified by nine o'clock tonight and we can
    consider this matter closed.  It is the only
    option.
```

The letter was unsigned. Tracy moaned lowly next to him as he crumpled up the paper.

"Dinner's getting cold."

She followed him into the kitchen. The dinner was delicious but neither of them noticed as they swallowed it in silence.

Halfway through the meal, they both looked up at each other when the sound of light tapping on the other door echoed through the room. Tracy held her breath and the hand holding the fork shook, sending some of her rice to the table.

"Take the plates into the next room," Dave said. She quickly scooped up both plates and rushed into the bedroom while he went over to the control panel on the far door. It had been outfitted with a special time lock, and he quickly punched a few of the keys until the panel beeped happily back at him. The LED display above the panel flashed the number twenty and then slowly counted down, ticking off the number of seconds before the door would unlock on it's own. Dave felt scared for the first time since he'd said yes to the proposition that they'd made him twelve years ago and he ran to the bedroom and closed the door behind him. It locked and he pressed his ear to it.

"Why did you run," she asked behind him. "What are they gonna…?"

"Shhhhhh!" he said and continued to listen.

There wasn't much to hear. Only one pair of feet entered, went quickly as far as the table and retreated again. He heard the far door swish shut and the beep as the autolock engaged. He looked up at the green light above the door.

The light was flickering.

Something, not a man, was lightly treading on the floor.

A snake?

That was one way to bring Ms. Baxter's contract to an end, he thought.

"What is it?" Tracy asked. "Is someone in there?"

"Not someone." His voice was flat; there wasn't any way he could say that without scaring her. She crept up behind him and gently placed a hand on his shoulder.

"Maybe if we just leave it alone…"

He turned back to her, incredulous. "Our food's in there, remember?"

"Yeah, but if we just leave it alone for a while, maybe they'll get tired of waiting and take it away. Maybe they'll…"

It scratched lightly on the door. Tracy gasped and Dave opened the door before she could say another word.

Standing there was a kitten.

It was white with patches of light brown fur. It looked up at them with cold wonder.

It was the cat that she wanted, that neither of them had gotten around to asking for.

A line from Tracy's note sprang into Dave's mind. "…I don't

know what our friend has told you…"

Oh yes, you do.

* * *

She called it Muckle.

It was with them for two weeks, the most maddening two weeks of their lives. They talked in low voices and then shushed each other the few times one of them forgot. The stress of having to speak in whispers, of knowing that someone was listening, began to weigh heavily on them. When the urge to cave into their demands rose inside him, he went into the control room to watch the monitors and daydream over the buttons while she would read her book. When she got tired of reading, she'd play with Muckle while he picked up the book and started going through it.

Every few hours, they had great sex.

Afterwards, whispering and dozing. Eventually, they'd separate again.

They ate in silence. Only Muckle would make noise. Dave would shush her and then silently chide himself for it.

On the sixth day, after the sex, they both laid in bed, panting. Muckle, on the floor, grabbed hold of the corner of the sheet that was hanging off the bed with her teeth and tried to pull it off. Tracy pulled back.

"Muckle, No."

"Shhhhhhh." said Dave.

"Oh, stop it! What are they going to learn about us by me disciplining the cat?" Tracy rolled away from him.

"You're right, I'm sorry."

Tracy didn't say anything. Dave rolled over to her side. "I said I was sorry."

"I'm sorry, too."

Dave continued to speak in a whisper, reminding her to do the same.

"You're sorry you came here."

"Yes."

"You're sick of me."

"I… not re…"

"You're sick of me."

"Kinda'."

"You're probably even sick of the cat, aren't you?"

At that moment, Muckle tried pulling the sheet again. Tracy pulled back ferociously.

"Yes, Yes, YES!"

"Keep your voice down!" Dave said, not realizing that his own voice was rising.

"What are they gonna hear that they don't already know: that we fuck a lot? That we're trying to find a way to beat those bastards and there isn't one? That one of us is ten seconds away from opening that Goddamned door and being finished with the whole thing? Is that what you're afraid of?" She looked up at him and said, "How did you get me into this mess?"

Dave felt his face grow hot. "I didn't know you when you walked through that door. They're the ones that brought you here!"

Tracy held him with her cold eyes. "You wanted a woman and they found me. Just like I wanted a cat and Muckle showed up. And now we're all stuck here!"

"Alright, that's it!" Dave jumped out of bed, not even stopping to put his underwear on.

Tracy suddenly looked frightened. "What are you doing?"

His only answer was to charge to her side and grab her arm. He yanked and pulled her out of the bed, both her and the sheets crashing to the floor. She had barely found her feet when he was pulling her across the room.

Then he began shouting. "Alright! You guys win! You can have her!"

"Dave, what are you doing?" She swung to grab for the bedpost and missed. Muckle jumped back from the pair and hissed. Dave pulled her closer to the door.

"I've had enough of her... and the fucking cat, too! You can take them both!"

"Dave!"

"She'll be coming through the door in T minus five... four... three..."

"No!"

Dave swung for the button that would open the door, but Tracy grabbed his arm and screamed fiercely. She thrashed, slapping his face and disturbing his grip. She broke free and sprinted into the far corner, huddling down and hiding her face in her arms.

Dave could hear her crying. A moment later, he heard the boots running down the corridor, heading for them.

He lifted his head and shouted, "Sorry, false alarm!"

Immediately, the boots in the outer corridor slid to a halt. He thought he heard someone sigh in frustration before the footsteps slowly retreated.

Dave slowly went to her, picking up the kitten along the way. He crouched down to the crying woman and the cat's paw flicked her shoulder. She sniffed and looked at them.

"She wants her Mommy," Dave said.

Tracy looked at the kitten, scrunched up her nose and took her from him, cradling the fluffy beast tightly.

He rubbed Tracy's feet for ten minutes and she stopped crying. Then he got bored and went to read her book while she played with the cat.

Eight days later, Muckle was dead.

It was Tracy's turn to make dinner. She and Muckle were in the kitchen while Dave was sitting on the bed, engrossed in one of the Don's great adventures. Tracy was preparing hamburger, the fanciest thing they had. After the false alarm, whoever it was that brought the food stopped bringing them the choice cuts, no matter how many times they asked for them. Dave had written email after email and had shouted at the ceiling, but it was always hamburger in the end. Even when he'd slyly ended his last email with a barely veiled threat concerning the buttons, hamburger still showed up on the kitchen table.

He'd heard their words loud and clear: *You want the good stuff again? All you have to do is…*

So it was hamburger.

And Dave was thinking of how sick he was of hamburger when

Tracy screamed.

"Dave! Oh my God! Come Quick!"

He leaped from the bed and charged into the kitchen. There, he found Tracy standing over Muckle, her hands wanting to reach for the animal as it writhed in agony but they hung haltingly over it. Muckle let out a sound that could only be the feline version of a scream. Both Dave and Tracy blocked their ears and shivered at the sound.

"What should I do?"

"Do?" He looked up at her. "I don't even know what happened!"

Tracy's hands still hovered over her ears, prepared for another scream. Her throat was closing up in panic. "I don't know either! She was fine! She was scrambling across the floor to get a bit of hamburger that I dropped and..."

Dave nearly fell backwards in shock. "She ate the food that you were..."

And then Muckle screamed again and Tracy joined her.

Are you guys enjoying this?

He sprang up and looked into the frying pan that held their dinner, the ground-up hamburger. It looked like it should've looked: brown and greasy. But a small bit had gone down Muckle's throat and...

Muckle screamed again, this time weakly.

"Oh Dave, do something! She's suffering!"

The frying pan was in his hand. Without a second thought, he dumped the meat into the sink and turned, raising it high above his head.

Muckle looked up at it, vomited slightly, and died.

The kitchen had a small hatchway for refuse and that was how

Muckle the kitten escaped their prison.

* * *

They stopped going into the kitchen. They both realized that there was no point in going back in for any reason: all the new food was suspect and neither of them could face it. They broke out a small container that had leftover potatoes from the night before and let the door close behind them forever. While Tracy munched a potato, Dave took a marker and wrote on the door:

HERE LIES

MUCKLE

?-2086

SHE DIDN'T KNOW WHAT SHE WAS GETTING INTO.

R.I.P.

They drank from the bathroom sink and tried to tell themselves that those who brought the food had no way of getting to the tap water. They drank and nothing happened to them.

The potatoes didn't last very long.

On the thirteenth day after Muckle's death, Dave and Tracy kissed each other for what they assumed would be the last time. They sat in the corner, feeling no energy to get into the bed. They sat in the corner like two old soldiers waiting for their trench to be overrun. Indeed, Dave thought he could hear the pacing of boots outside the door.

The two spoke in whispers, not because they didn't want to be heard but because it was all they had the strength for.

"They'll come in as soon as it's over," he said.

"I thought they couldn't get in?"

"They'll find a way. They'll probably blow the door or something."

"Then why don't they do it now?"

Dave fell silent for a moment.

"I don't know."

Tracy coughed before answering her own question.

"Maybe they're hedging their bets. Maybe they think you'll turn me over before it's too late." She looked up at him weakly. "You wanna?"

"No." The word was out of his mouth before she stopped speaking.

Tracy used up a Herculean amount of strength to smile. "I guess I just have that kind of face that you can't walk away from."

The two of them sat there, breathing in and out, almost in sync. He took hold of her hand and squeezed it.

"Do you take me?" he asked.

"I do. Do you take me?"

"Yeah."

And they kissed. Their heads swam and neither of them remembered it five seconds after it was over. Tracy's head fell backwards.

"I'm tired."

"Get some rest," he said, "there's something I have to do."

But she was already asleep. He looked at her deeply, saw her chest moving up and down and realized that it was indeed sleep. But it wouldn't be for long. He'd only decided on his course of action a moment before.

He gingerly snaked his arm from behind her head, letting her rest against the wall. Taking a deep breath, he reached out, grabbed the dresser and strained to pull himself up. As soon as he was up, his head felt like it was spinning and he grabbed onto the dresser as hard as he could, but his knees were turning to water.

Only a few steps... that's all I got...

Seven steps, as it turned out. Seven long, lurching steps that took him out of the bedroom and halfway to the control panel before he collapsed onto his face. Blackness swarmed over him.

Have I been asleep, he thought when he lifted his head again. Time had definitely passed but whether it was ten minutes or twelve hours, he had no way of knowing. Part of him (hell, all of him) wanted to go back to check on Tracy, to see if she was still alive, and to collapse right beside her if she wasn't.

But that wasn't why he'd come into the control room in the first place.

He savored those words - *control room* - and used them as the strength he needed to crawl across the floor and pull himself into the chair which, on wheels, nearly rolled away from him. After what seemed to him like forever, he was sitting in his old chair and looking at the buttons.

The dusty buttons.

Each with a label above it.

Tokyo... Bonn... Washington, D.C.... Buenos Aires... Brussels...

Blackpool... Rio de Janeiro... Juno... Topeka... Canberra... Boston... Cairo... Bangkok... Bangor... London... Bagdad... Moscow...

Each button a destination.

Dave looked up at the monitors. On them, the news anchors were spouting and the politicians were blathering. He hated them. They were the one's who created this room. They were the one's who found him and placed him here. They'd found him women when he wanted them and disposed of them when he was finished. They'd found Tracy and brought her here. And now...

They think I've gone soft, just because I wanted to keep her. They think I won't...

Blackness swarmed around his eyes again. He shook his head clear.

Into the deep... the color is black...

They could get food, enough food to last them forever. It was all behind the steel door, the one that would open as soon as he...

At least, they told him the rations were there.

Maybe they lied...

Too late to worry about that now.

He looked up at the red light. It was still dark. Dave knew that was the last time he would ever look at the light. He focused his attention on the buttons.

London... Bagdad... Moscow... Washington D.C.

How nice that they'd put those four side by side.

* * *

As lovely as music, as soft as a breeze, the voice slowly whirled in her head.

Fortune is guiding our affairs better than we ourselves could have wished. Do you see over yonder, my friend Sancho Panza, thirty or more huge giants?

It felt like a light had gone on somewhere inside of her where she was certain there would only be darkness. A pinprick... a hope...

I intend to do battle with them and slay them: with their spoils we shall begin to be rich, for this is a righteous war and the removal of so foul a brood from off the face of the Earth is a service God will bless.

She climbed up, reaching and grasping up and up towards the light. She had to reach it and find out how the story ended. The voice got louder as her eyes fluttered open.

"Take care, sir," said Dave, sitting next to her and reading from her book, "those over there are not giants, but windmills."

"Dave?"

He looked from the book to her pale face. Her voice was so quiet that he almost believed it had come from Heaven.

"I couldn't wake you at first. I didn't know what to do." His voice was choked.

"Dave," she said, trying and failing to lift herself off the floor. "I... my head... I'm..."

"Here, eat this."

In his hand was an open can of beef stew. For the first time since she'd woken, Tracy breathed through her nose and smelled the hot gravy. Her eyes shifted to the burning Sterno can nearby.

Dave dipped a fork into the can, came up with a piece of warm, spiced meat and fed it to Tracy, who didn't take her eyes off him. He fed her two more bites before her stomach began to cramp. She rolled over and moaned.

"It'll pass. I felt it too," he said.

After a moment, she rolled back and simply looked at him. When her look became too difficult to meet, he read aloud from the book again.

"You're going to read the whole thing to me?"

"Why not?"

He read a few more lines before she interrupted again.

"And when the book is finished?"

"There are others."

Dave read to her and Tracy found herself smiling as she easily fell back into the story, the grand tale of the brave but misguided knight who did not shirk from the windmills and, in the end, was true to his Dulcinea.

PUT THE BOOK BACK WHERE YOU FOUND IT.
DO NOT TURN THE PAGE!

Into The Deep... The Color Is Black...

Anonymous

1

The Memorial Café stood across the street from the entrance to Juniper Hill cemetery. It had been there so long that people sometimes wondered if the café was named because of its proximity to Juniper Hill or if the city had put the cemetery there to enhance the café. As far as the locals knew, it was one of few businesses that had been in existence for all of their lives and even those who never crossed its threshold subconsciously found the presence of the café to be of great comfort. The fact that it had kept its doors open for all these years gave the old building a certain resilient pride: stores at the mall might come and go, but certain things remained even in the craziest of economies. Of course, the café's persistent good fortune had always depended on visitors to Juniper Hill deciding that a nice, quiet place to sit and reflect on the nature of life and loss was just the thing they needed (that and a piping-hot coffee). The dead never moved out of Juniper Hill, their friends and family never failed to visit them, and the café never went out of business. You didn't have to be bereaved to go to the Memorial Café, but it helped.

So year after year, the café opened its door to the grieving and down-at-heart. The coffee and tea were always hot and sweet, the small cakes were soft and fresh, and no one noticed how, once a year, something horrible happened there.

2

On September 9th, 2011, Gillian Gardner was sitting on the grass in front of a grave, not caring about the damp ground or how wet her pants were getting. Every time she lifted her gaze from the grass that she was absently pulling at, all she could see in front of her was the stone with the two year-old inscription:

𝔇𝔢𝔫𝔫𝔦𝔰 𝔍𝔞𝔪𝔢𝔰 𝔠𝔞𝔰𝔰𝔞𝔟𝔢𝔱𝔢𝔰

1986-2009

𝔅𝔢𝔩𝔬𝔟𝔢𝔡 𝔤𝔯𝔞𝔫𝔡𝔰𝔬𝔫 𝔬𝔣 𝔑𝔞𝔫𝔢𝔱𝔱𝔢 𝔅𝔬𝔶𝔩𝔢

She wished the words "Beloved boyfriend of Gillian Gardner" could've been included on the stone, but "Nana Nan" (as Dennis had referred to her, which had always sounded to Gillian like a brat's taunt) wasn't about to splash out the extra cash on a girl who had started dating her grandson only four months before he wrapped his car around a tree after a night of drinking with his friends. She'd sympathized with the grief-stricken girl, but four months of necking in cars wasn't *blood*. *Blood* was what connected people and, as far as Nana Nan was concerned, she was the only blood in her grandson's brief life.

He was inside me… is that connected enough for you?

Gillian sniffed and stole a look at the stone directly to the right of Dennis's: Nana Nan had outlasted her grandson by less than a year.

Four months, Nana Nan? Four fucking months?

Gillian had first lost her heart to Dennis in the seventh grade; back when braces and glasses had kept her from ever approaching the already mature and muscular head of the soccer team. She'd spent many a Saturday watching his young and agile body sneak yet one more goal into the visitors' net. She'd jumped up and cheered with all her heart as he celebrated yet another goal on the field: she would've cheered him if he'd been stuck on the bench for the entire game.

Notice me… please notice me…

And finally he did: by her junior year, the braces had come off, she'd found a pair of glasses that suited her face better, and the entire school had discovered what a beautiful voice she had after her stint in the school's production of *No No, Nanette*. Her heart had melted the first time he took a moment to acknowledge her as she shyly snaked her way down the hallway to her next class. He'd been going steady with another girl at the time, but something in his eyes had impressed on her that someday…

You and me, sweet little thing… just you wait: once I grow up and leave these silly little flirtations behind me, then it will be you and me for life… just you wait… just you see…

And four months before his death, the waiting had come to an end: bumping into him at a bar with her contacts firmly in place and her hair highlighted to near perfection had finally captured his obsession. And oh… to be his obsession…

I'm at the center of a raging sea... rocked but safe within my true love's arms... I suffocate, but I don't mind... touch me and breathe into me... I'm nothing without...

Beautiful, with a heart about to burst with happiness...

Thank you for loving me...

...and then gone with no warning.

Gillian took a deep breath and struggled to stand up again. She knew that she'd been there long enough: she didn't want to be found collapsed forward on the grave sleeping like she was last year. No, her parents and dearest friends were always telling her that she had to move on with her life and she had agreed. The thrice-weekly visits during the first year had decreased to once a month and she was finally allowing herself to look around at the men who surrounded her at work and think about what it might be like to spend an evening with one of them. But her heart was still attached to Dennis and she wondered how long it would be before it stopped hurting.

She turned, walked down the path to the front gate and found herself on the sidewalk. She was just about to walk up the block to where her car was parked, when the strength to walk drained out of her legs.

Come on... time to get back to the real world... just like you did last month, remember?

Gillian looked around her and spotted the Memorial Café sitting across the street with its red neon sign declaring to the grey world outside that it was open for business.

That's kind of tacky, she thought; using a cemetery as a tie-in for your coffee shop. Still, she wouldn't have to go back to real-life just yet and a coffee did sound enticing.

The street wasn't busy and Gillian got across it easily. Pushing back the usual apprehension that many feel when entering a new place for the first time, she stepped into the café.

Although it had not been all that bright outside (the clouds, as if in mourning for Dennis as well, refused to let sunshine break through them), Gillian stood at the door and squinted as her eyes adjusted to the dim light. The walls were painted mostly black with only touches of grey and purple to dispel the illusion that she'd fallen into the inner-reaches of Sylvia Path's head. The ceiling lamps were evidently on a dimmer that was kept at a very low setting. The only real light shone from a bare bulb hanging directly over the counter. A large woman behind the counter barely looked up at her as she entered, mostly content to lean on the counter in a bored half-stupor. It was more than the three customers, scattered at separate tables throughout the room, had done. With her eyes adjusting further, Gillian could see that each table had its own lamp, but only one was switched on. At that table sat a young man leaning over a book so that his long hair obscured his face. He was dressed almost entirely in black as were the other two customers, who sat at their darkened tables staring off into space and listening to the music.

Oh, the music: thick, dark and gloomy. Strings, woodwinds and synthesizers playing in minor keys drifted from the speakers on the walls. It wasn't loud, but it didn't need to be: each depressing note fell like sludge into the room. Gillian nearly turned and walked out again when the woman behind the counter asked, "Would you like a coffee or tea?"

Gillian slowly crossed the distance to the counter and looked up at the chalkboard displaying the menu. It was difficult considering that the bulb that illuminated it had no shade and was shining in her eyes.

"Have you been up at the cemetery?" the large woman asked.

"Um… yeah. Doesn't everyone who comes here come from…"

"Nope," she answered with a sigh before nodding towards the rest of her clientele. "They just come here because they like it here. Weird, if you ask me." Gillian turned and noticed for the first time that all three customers were not just dressed in black, but were all wearing jackboots and had multiple piercings. All three had black hair and, now that her eyes were completely adjusted to the dimness, she could tell that they were all the victims of shoddy dye-jobs.

"They just sit and listen to the music, read a bit, buy coffee and never make trouble. Business is business. I'm sorry for your loss, by the way." She said the last like she was sorry that Gillian had stubbed her toe on the way in.

"Thank you…"

"Call me Sophie."

Gillian had not been seeking any name to call the woman by. There didn't seem much point in starting a first name relationship with a two hundred and fifty pound woman whom she would probably never see again. "Thank you, Sophie, but I was visiting someone who's been gone for a couple of years now and…"

"Don't matter," Sophie said. "This is your first time here and that qualifies you for the 'Bereavement Special.'"

Gillian wasn't sure if she'd heard right. "The what?"

"You get a dollar off your first large cup of anything that you want. And a double-shot of whipped cream if you order cocoa." Sophie stood there, looking at the girl's face and knowing that she was wondering if she should storm out in a huff or not. Many new customers found the notion that their loss had the upside of a discounted coffee repellent and Sophie was used to them telling her so. That was okay; people drowning in grief sometimes needed to explode at another person and the Bereavement Special gave them the opportunity. She knew enough to stand there and wait, without making a sound or changing the expression on her face, while Gillian made up her mind.

"Just something hot and strong, please." And then a bit lower, "You don't have anything stronger to put in it, do you?"

"Sorry, Miss, but this is just a coffee shop," Sophie said, but Gillian thought that the woman had given her the briefest of winks. "Name?"

"I'm Jill."

"No, what was his or her name?"

"Oh... Cassavetes, Dennis Cassavetes."

Sophie immediately turned and walked down the length of the counter, fetching a small stepladder and bringing it back underneath something that Gillian had not noticed before, a large map of Juniper Hill Cemetery. She reached under the counter and brought out a three-ring binder, flipping through and repeating Dennis's name. After a moment, she replaced the binder, climbed up two steps of the ladder and traced her

finger to the point that marked Dennis's final resting place. Gillian was

surprised to see the large woman stick a pin with a tiny paper flower

attached to it right next to her finger.

Sophie puffed a bit as she reached ground level. "I'll bring your

drink to you. Just sit anywhere you like. We've got lots of books, so

help yourself."

For the first time that day, Gillian was smiling. "Thank you,

Sophie."

Gillian chose a table close to the large bookcase that stretched the

entire length of the west wall, turned her table lamp on, and took in a real

good look at her surroundings: for the first time, she noticed that there

were empty picture frames of brown and purple hanging on the walls,

showing only the black wall behind them. The only thing on the wall

that was not an empty frame was a large painting, at least two feet by

five, of a bare willow tree bending in a strong wind. None of the other

customers had broken their concentration when she'd walked past them

or turned on her lamp. She could see the girl's profile and the myriad of

studs that stuck out from her face; her head swayed ever so slightly as if

in rhythm with the tuneless dirge that was playing. The boy at the other

darkened table had his back to Gillian, so she could not catch any details

about him at all. She stole a glance at the boy who was leaning

feverishly over a book; only two tables separated them so he was the

closest of the three to her. She could still not see his face clearly because

of his long hair, but she could see that his head and shoulders were bobbing up and down slightly as he read and, after hearing him sniff loudly, she imagined that he might be crying.

Well, that can't be a rare thing in a place like this.

With nothing else to look at in the dim room, Gillian turned her attention to the bookcase and squinted to read the titles from her table. She pivoted her table lamp up towards the closest of the books and the titles came into focus.

Just as I thought...

Sylvia Plath's name was the first one that jumped out at her, followed by *The Tragedy of Hamlet, The Prince Of Denmark* and *The Long Walk* by Stephen King. She'd read that one years before when it was first released under the name of Richard Bachman and, if her memory served her well, it was just the type of book that should be sitting on a shelf in a place like the Memorial Café: a harrowing story capped with a bleak ending. It made sense; this was a place of deep grief and contemplation because the customers were in pain. There would be no Douglas Adams or Christopher Moore on the shelves because that just wasn't what the café was here for: you want to cheer up, go somewhere else.

She got up and was about to pull the Plath collection free when a larger, leather-bound tome caught her eye. It looked dustier than its neighbors and the gold lettering on the binding was caught by her lamplight and sparkled briefly:

**M
e
m
o
r
i
a
l

T
a
l
e
s**

Big Sophie must have published her own book… or maybe the title's just a coincidence.

Whatever the truth was, the title was promising and it looked to be the only thing in the vicinity that might be completely new to her. Not wanting to search all the books in the dim light, she pulled the book out. A puff of dust blew in her face and she waited for the sneezy feeling to pass. Waving the rest of the dust away, she sat back down at the table, placed the book under the lamp and cracked it open.

When she slammed the cover shut a couple of seconds later, the other three customers jumped slightly at the noise. They all looked at her, rolled their eyes, and went back to what they were doing before she interrupted them. Gillian noticed none of this; she simply sat in her chair, a spooky feeling running across her shoulders.

She might have sat there for the rest of her life if Sophie hadn't come up to place a steaming hot mug in front of her. Now it was Gillian's turn to jump.

"I'm sorry, Honey," the large woman said, "I didn't mean to startle you."

Gillian looked at the cup in front of her for a moment; when she looked back up, she could see that Sophie was waiting for some type of acknowledgement.

"Is this your book?"

Gillian was about to show Sophie the cover, but the large woman cut her off.

"Nothing here is mine, sweetie," she said, "I ain't the owner or nothin'; I just work here."

Sophie started to turn away, but Gillian stopped her with a sentence. "My name's written in this!"

She wasn't sure, but she thought the large woman took a moment too long to turn back. "What's your name?"

"Gillian Gardner," she said, and she opened the book and held up the first page to Sophie, who squinted in the dim light. Three questions were written on the page:

Who does this book belong to?

Will you promise to take care of it?

Will you promise to read it all the way through?

After the first question was the handwritten name of "Jill Gardner." The other two answered in the affirmative.

"Honey, what are you writing in our books for?"

Gillian looked back at the large woman, not believing what she heard. 'I didn't write in it; I opened it up and found my name written in it *in my own handwriting!*"

"I guess that proves it, doesn't it?" She turned her back on Gillian before she could give an answer. She was threading her way, as best as her fat thighs would let her, between the tables back to the counter. Gillian wanted to call to her that she didn't even have a pen on her to deface the book, but the eyes of the other creepy customers were turned to her and the words hitched in her throat. Here she was, alone in a café and ready to make a scene about something that was undeniably weird but not something she could actually blame anyone for.

What the Hell could she possibly have done… guessed my name and wrote it in the book before I got here?

And was the name "Jill Gardner" all that unique? It might have been a hell of a coincidence, but it wasn't exactly Archemedes Ambercrombie, was it?

My name's in this book…

Gillian turned the page, noted that she was indeed reading the book by the light of a single bulb (as the book commanded her to do), and turned the page again.

3

*The sun was going down and the light amongst the
trees was dimming, but Bobby walked slowly through the
forest, looking apprehensively around yet another tall oak...*

*...His good, booming voice bellowed the same
command as before. "Lower the drawbridge! Raise the
portcullis! Welcome the King!"*

*In the stranger's hands was a box covered with a velvet
cloth. He held it out proudly like a calling card...*

*...After a minute of chewing, she swallowed and two
short bones poked out of her smiling lips, which she
nonchalantly spat across the floor.*

"I don't like the bones," she said simply.

*Eddie, lying on his back and trying to blink away the
blood in his eyes...*

*...The only sound in the apartment came from his
crunching teeth and the hiss of the boiling water. He heard
nothing from the woman in his closet. A brief thought about
Mommy's Mr. Scratch occurred to him, but he didn't let it
bother him; in fact, he felt warmed by the idea that he'd beaten
Mommy with the thing that she feared the most...*

*...Sophie gingerly lifted the mousetrap, the mouse
swaying limply in its jaws, and quietly chanted a bit more
gibberish. She slowly lifted the wire clamp and released the
dead mouse from the trap, where it fell with a soft plop onto
Limbaugh's face...*

4

Gillian lifted her eyes from the page and looked towards the counter. The light had shifted since she'd sat down; sunlight raked the counter and illuminated the large woman who loitered behind it. She listlessly rearranged the mugs stacked along the counter in the time-worn style of a worker who has been trained to look busy when business was slow. She raised her eyes momentarily to Gillian and, if she noticed the look on Gillian's face, she showed no hint of discomfort.

Her name was the same as the girl in the story, not to mention her weight. And then there were the references to the café she was sitting in at that very moment with...

Gillian shifted her gaze to the portrait of the willow bending in the wind.

It was hanging, two feet by five (just like in the story), on the opposite wall, right in front of her.

She flipped a few pages back to find the title of the story:

Teach Yourself Satanism

(2001)

Hieronymus Scratch

Hieronymus Scratch? What the Hell kind of name was that?

"You need a fresh cup, Honey?"

Neither of the other remaining customers stirred at the sound of Sophie's voice. The Plath scholar had left at some point during the day, leaving the two Goths sitting at their tables and bobbing listlessly to something over the speakers that sounded like a stew of moaning monks, a short-circuiting Moog and an asthmatic moose in labor.

Neither of them had stirred: they both were looking at her even before Sophie spoke.

Gillian picked up her mug: not a single drop from the cold mug had been drunk.

"I'm fine," she said.

Sophie was about to go back to looking busy when she suddenly noticed the other two customers looking at Gillian. With a throat-clearing grunt, they both went back to staring at the ceiling.

Gillian didn't take her eyes off the other two customers until a clunk on her table made her realize that Sophie was again standing next to her. A small bottle of whiskey was now sitting next to her mug.

"I thought you said that this was just a coffee shop," Gillian said as Sophie scooped up the cold mug.

"It was when you walked in."

Sophie went back to her counter. Gillian went back to her book.

5

...He didn't know her name, the phrase "Pink Kid" went through his mind whenever he thought of her, and that was exactly the way he wanted it. Not that knowing her name would've made what he would eventually do any more difficult; those sort of second thoughts were reserved for those who had a conscience to bother them...

...Anyway, the girl is stomping right in front of me, the room is boiling, the stench of mutant sweat is getting nauseating and this girl suddenly drops her head, takes one look at me and points at me without breaking step. Did she not see Miranda sitting next to me? Maybe she did and maybe not, but before I could do anything...

...Tracy found herself smiling as she easily fell back into the story, the grand tale of the brave but misguided knight who did not shirk from the windmills and, in the end, was true to his Dulcinea.

PUT THE BOOK BACK WHERE YOU FOUND IT. DO NOT TURN THE PAGE!

6

Gillian stared at the page in front of her for ten minutes, reading and rereading the two sentences that had stopped her breath cold the first time she read them.

What the Hell kind of book is this?

A simple wish to escape the world for the span of time that it takes to drink a cup of coffee had somehow led to this: a book that didn't want the reader to finish it, even though her own handwriting on the first page had already promised that she would. Her fingers toyed with the edge of the page, playing at flipping it over.

She burped slightly and a strange taste came up her throat and sizzled her nose. When she recognized the flavor, she looked to the bottle that Sophie had left on her table: three-quarters empty.

She peeked behind her and out the window where, last that she remembered, there was daylight shining through. Immediately, she looked at her watch.

7:28

"You alright, Honey?" It was Sophie, large as life and twice as shocking, suddenly standing in front of her. She never heard the fat woman approach.

"I…" Gillian began before she took a look around. "Where is everybody?"

"Went home," she said, swaggering her head slightly. "I'll probably be able to close early tonight, thanks to you."

"Me?"

"They left because of you."

"Me? What the Hell did I do?"

Sophie looked aside for a moment, choosing her words. "Well… it wasn't anything you did, exactly. It was more of… the way you were." She smiled down at the girl, apparently content to let the matter rest at that.

"I was just… sitting here!"

"…and breathing."

"What?"

"Noisily. And the last one who left said… Honey, do you know what an aura is?"

Gillian couldn't believe what she was hearing. "Excuse me?"

"Nevermind. Finish up: the sooner you're done, the sooner I can close up."

"Finish up what?"

Sophie smiled and went back to the counter. Gillian looked down at the book with its written warning staring up at her.

Put the book back where you found it. Do not turn the page!

Gillian turned the page.

She read two pages, not believing what she was reading, and slammed the book shut.

Dennis's name is in here... Nana Nan... all my thoughts... my feelings up there in the cemetery... how could it all be here?

She looked around the café and saw that she was alone; even Sophie had deserted her. Instinctively, she reached for the three-quarters empty bottle and made it fully empty.

Gillian turned back to the window and saw a young couple passing in front of the café. She started to rise from her chair, but then she saw them quite deliberately change their direction, just enough to make it clear they were steering clear of the café, without any change of attitude. They continued to talk and joke with each other while avoiding getting too close to the café

.

Honey, do you know what an aura is?

Gillian looked down at her arms, confused. For a moment, she thought she saw something dark glowing just above her skin.

She blinked and it was gone.

Gillian sat up straight, afraid that she would be sick all over the table if she leaned over. The room fell out of focus and she felt herself swaying: somehow, the book had known what she was doing and thinking as she sat by Dennis's grave only a few hours before. No doubt, if she persisted in reading, she would read about herself deciding to visit the café and detail her most vivid thoughts about the woman behind the counter and the weird clientele.

She'd read about herself choosing this particular book.

She'd read about herself reading.

Maybe she'd even read all those stories all over again.

Eventually, she'd read about how she finally looked up and found herself all alone in the café, tipsy, scared and glowing with a poisoned aura.

And then she'd read...

What?

Gillian took a few deep breaths and allowed her vision to focus again... on the picture of the willow tree.

In that story... where Sophie ran here in her slippers... she saw that picture... and it moved...

She stood up and approached the painting, savoring the scuff of her shoes on the wooden floor as proof that she was tangibly still in the world. With her head spinning the way it was, she didn't know what to think.

The painting was actually a pen-and-ink drawing, but an expertly done one. A gale was evidently blowing from off to the right of the picture since the flaccid branches were caught in mid-gust pointing to the left. The grass, each blade distinct in the artist's meticulous style, was bending in the same direction. There were no birds in the scene as she could not imagine that they could survive taking flight in such a squall, but she thought she could see a few leaves just losing the fight of holding on for dear life. She shivered, almost feeling a gust of wind down her neck.

I did feel it!

She shook her head awake and found the name of the artist in the bottom right corner: Hieronymus Scratch.

A second later, the letters blew away in the wind.

Gillian gasped and stepped backwards, nearly stepping on the toes of the large woman standing behind her. When she turned, she realized that Sophie was looking at her with a hopeful expression.

"Did you read the whole book?"

Gillian shook her head. Sophie's face fell. She thought she could feel a breeze blowing against her again.

"I knew you wouldn't. None of them ever do. Of course, it might not make any difference in the end. But I always imagine that it might help… knowing what was going to happen."

Gillian stepped back from her. "There was a story about you…"

She nodded, sadly. "It was a few years ago when I saw what was happening here. I saw it through a cheap crystal ball that I bought in some two-bit store that doesn't exist anymore. I wanted to be the Devil's bride and I thought this place could help me find him. Well, I found something, but it didn't want me... at least, not the way it wants you."

Gillian felt cold; a wind was definitely blowing in the café. She stepped backwards as Sophie advanced.

"Did you read this far in the book?"

The frightened girl shook her head.

Sophie looked defeated. "Too bad... you might have seen this coming!"

Sophie suddenly lunged forward, grabbed Gillian and shoved her backwards into the painting. She felt it shatter behind her and then realized that she was falling into a deep hole, the walls of which turned to flesh and extended to embrace her.

The long, horrible scream of *NOOOOO* was swallowed as the hole enfolded her and gulped her down into its gullet.

Sophie stood there for a moment, reflecting on how many times she stood in that spot, before bending over and scooping up Gillian's shoes, which she had lost in all the excitement.

She knew that she would find the girl's pocketbook still at the table waiting for her to collect it, just as she knew that the book would not be there, having found its own way back onto the shelf.

As she trudged to the table, she muttered something under her breath:

"Deep... it must be... and... so dark... *black...*

The tunnel, like a great muscle, pressed down on her and edged her forward, forcing the breath out of her. She tried to think, but panicking was all she could manage as her burning lungs struggled to breathe. With her arms pressed by her side, she couldn't bring herself to grab onto anything solid. She went rigid, felt her head swoon and closed her eyes.

Suddenly, the pressure all around her released and she felt herself ejected into clear space. As she drew her first breath, she tumbled and came to rest heavily on an incline of dirt and stone. She slid back slightly, the result of her being covered with a thin film of goo. She laid there for a moment, just listening to the pebbles shifting around her, before daring to open her eyes.

There was light coming from behind her; not much of it, but enough for her to see the hole in the rock face just a few feet above her. It had closed over and all that was left was a depression in the stone. She reached up and touched the solid membrane: it shivered under her finger but remained steadfast. She had come from there and could tell that, if she was going to get back, it would not be by that route.

Groaning with every ache, Gillian painfully got to her feet, noticing for the first time that her shoes were gone. Nothing seemed broken but every muscle screamed and the feel of stickiness on her skin and in her hair made her want to vomit. Shaking her head clear, she tried to concentrate only on the space around her.

What she could see told her that she was in more of a cave than a room or chamber. What little that was illuminated looked rocky and rough hewn. She could see no ceiling above her. Beneath her feet she felt uneven gravel biting into her soles.

And despite the light, all of it was black, as if some demented new-wave artist had splashed an ocean of black paint over everything. There was an artificial feel to it, as if it had all been done for her.

"Hello?" she said, not too loudly, uncertain if she really wanted to be heard by whatever had brought her to this place. Surprisingly, there was no echo; her voice fell flat a few feet in front of her.

And then there was the light coming from the stone archway in the opposite cave wall, an archway that would dwarf her once she stood underneath it.

I'm not going to get anywhere near it... I'm going to...

"Hello?" she called again, this time a bit louder. Hugging herself, she hobbled forward. "Where am I? Please, if somebody..."

Through the archway, as she got closer, she heard footsteps and what she thought might be a human voice. Gillian abandoned all reservations and ran to the archway, shouting the whole time.

"Please! I don't know where I am! I fell down a... I don't know what it was! I need help! Whoever you are, I need..."

Something fast, strong and hairy dove into her stomach and knocked her back ten feet, where she landed flat on her back, feeling it break in three places. The creature howled and jumped up and down on her stomach, its claws digging into her flesh with every trounce.

"Stop that right now!"

It was a woman's voice, cracked but still authoritative, that stopped the beast. It looked back at the figure standing backlit in the archway, growled resentfully, and stepped off Gillian's prone body. It waddled obediently back to the woman's outstretched hand, pausing only once to look back at the broken body that was not broken enough for its liking.

Gillian gasped for breath, felt nothing below her shoulder blades, and knew she was dead. All it would take was a moment more of strangulation and then...

"Come here. I'll try not to let him hurt you again."

Something swept down Gillian's body, warming her before the pain in her ribs started. She took a good, full breath of air and let it out with a moan. Way back in her mind, she was vaguely glad that she could bend her knees and wiggle her toes again, but she hurt so much that all she could do with her newly-mobile body was curl it up into a ball and cry.

"You! Get in there and wait for me," she heard the woman say, followed by the creature's footsteps slowly retreating. She continued to sob as she felt hands grasp her around the shoulders.

"Get up," the woman whispered in her ear. "I know it hurts, but I also know you can get up; injuries don't last long here, only the pain. You can't stay here."

Between sobs: "Wanna... go back..."

"Only forward from here. Come on."

The woman helped Gillian to her feet; every joint in her body creaked like squeaky door hinges. She raised her head and saw through her red eyes a face that had compassion breaking through the coldness that an impossible existence had forced upon it. She had no strength left and wanted to collapse against the woman, but she was held firmly and upright in strong arms.

"What's your name?" the woman asked.

"Jill Gardner."

"I'm Becky Dyne. You probably won't remember my name, but I'll bet you've read it recently. Rebecca Dyne, remember?"

Becky Dyne coaxed a few steps out of Gillian's legs through the archway.

"I'm sorry about what Bobby did to you," she said. "He doesn't know any better."

8

They called it "Home." It was, after all, where they lived. And would continue to live and live and live and live and live.

Once Becky Dyne explained who she was, and jogged Gillian's memory about Bobby, it wasn't hard to see and understand who the others were.

The naked man with the haunted eyes had the exact face that she pictured belonging to Professor Hunter Westlake, the time-traveling scientist from "Broken Record." The man stalking him from behind also had the same exact face and when he raised a revolver and blew his doppelganger's brains out, Gillian nearly broke free of Becky's grasp. Her eyes followed the man's blood and brain debris falling into the shining pit and she screeched in horror. But when she looked up again, the killer had taken his victim's place at the side of the pit, oblivious to the shadow growing closer and more menacing behind him with every step, ready to feel the bullet he had fired into his nemesis's head only a moment before.

All round the pit, nearly obscured by the blinding light shining out of it, were other figures that, until only that moment, she had only seen before in her mind's eye: the squeezed and broken head of the woman who had died from having her skull forced through the banister was staring into the pit with a dumb anticipation, Queen J held a mirror in front of her and forced herself to see the beauty of her scalded head through her tears, the starving Dave and Tracy lay in each other's arms, willing each other to keep living, Jeremy Van Dyke squeezed a moaning and drooling child to his chest, futilely willing a brain into the child before its mother walked into the room, and the man who was reduced to ragged flesh hanging off stained bones could be no other than Eduardo, victim of a ginger-haired cannibal. If his story was to be believed, there was no reason to pity him his agonies, but Jamyn had neglected to finish off his tear ducts, and they were still letting him pour out his every agony as another strip of his flesh was torn away.

Above it all was the glorious and ecstatic moaning of the Mistress hanging from her hooks, her flesh burning and turning to boils in the heat above the pit. She screamed in orgasmic relief as every drop of sweat and pus dripped and sizzled into the vapors below her suspended body.

All the while, little Bobby ran around snarling, all fangs and claws, nipping at the fingers of people who were hanging on to the edge of the pit, hanging down and screaming from the immense heat that flickered up and roasted their legs. The heat kept the lost, flesh-covered skeletons clinging fiercely to the edge, no matter how ravenously Bobby chewed away at their fingers. Sometimes, he got bored and went after the puppy-sized rats that scurried all over.

Moans, yelps, screams: there was no silence in the vicinity of the pit.

Becky held Gillian firmly just as she felt herself feeling faint; she felt Becky's hand lightly slapping her cheek to counter the effect of the fumes emanating from the pit.

"What's going on?" She felt faint again, her head spinning around to take in the bright red light that filled the cavern. Only the nibble of a rat at her ankle brought her focus back again.

"You've been caught, just like I was. I'm sorry... but this is it for you."

Instantly, she kicked her hardened foot out to repel Bobby as it dove at their shins. She'd done this many times before, kicking and yelling so many times that the creature feared of losing one of its precious teeth in pursuit of something tasty to chew on. Bobby took a few steps back, whimpered in frustration, and focused his attention on one pair of hands that were trying to lift themselves further out of the pit.

It charged and the dreaded thing slid back into the pit with an unholy howl.

Gillian pressed herself deeper into Becky's flesh, hoping to somehow be absorbed into the woman's body and be safe. As she took

one more look around at the misery surrounding her, a flash of hope
came to her.

"I used to sleepwalk…"

"This is real," Becky said, enunciating into her ear so that Gillian
would understand. "You did nothing wrong; you don't deserve to be
here. In a way, I caused this."

Gillian wrapped her arms around the woman and moaned into her
chest.

"At least, I'm the one that made that little monster over there:
little Bobby with the human eyes and the fangs. Maybe that's why I've
been sent here. But…" Her strong voice faltered into a strangled
whimper.

Gillian guessed correctly. "Does it matter?"

A flash of intense heat baked their faces and the cavern was filled
with the screams of those who hung from their fingernails. The two
women cowered and Becky waited until she was sure Gillian could hear
her above the moans before she spoke again.

"It's coming… and it's coming for you." She kissed Gillian's
forehead. "I can't help you… I… I have to get into the pit."

Almost immediately, Becky pushed the young girl away from her,
so suddenly and violently that Gillian stumbled backwards, her look of
surprise never leaving her face. Even as she crashed onto the rock floor,
she kept her eyes locked onto Becky as she edged backwards towards the
pit and, whimpering as the illuminated heat licked at her ankles, she
crouched down, grabbed a firm hold of a thin root running in the ground
in front of her, and gingerly lowered herself into the steaming pit, her

moans reaching a frenzy as she relaxed her body to accept the white-hot blaze.

A horrendous thud shook the cavern.

I'm not here… I'm not!

Another thud, same intensity. The fingers at the edge of the pit dug tighter into the dirt.

Gillian looked around her and realized that she had been left alone: the book's characters had scattered, the remaining souls, captured as she had been through the portrait, were in the pit, and even Bobby had scurried away.

She fell to her knees as the creature strode forward into the cavern; its breath blew fetid fumes into her face.

The boy who had willed the creature into existence (*Little HieRONNIEmus*) to set his mother straight about who was boss in that household, who had written his own story to punish his mother and never stopped his regiment of punishment until it swallowed any and all poor dreadful souls who fell into his path, who found enough strength and will to create a playground of suffering for which he could ensnare the innocent and twisted alike, rode upon the creature's scaly back into the cavern. The moans from the pit intensified; they all knew what was to come and they shrieked in unison.

But there was something more, a figure being dragged alongside the creature, led by a choke chain held by the child that left deep gouges on the figure's neck. The figure was trying to keep out of the way of the creature's gigantic feet, but the length of the chain kept him close and on the verge of strangulation. Finally, he stumbled forward, exhaustion making him nearly oblivious to his own suffering and, as the scaly creature planted itself in the chamber, the child took one last tug and forced the figure to his knees. The light from the pit illuminated the figure's blue and swollen face.

Gillian, who had been inching away, suddenly ran towards the figure.

"*DENNIS!*"

The figure shook his head, trying to warn her away, but Gillian paid no attention. She got down on her knees and threw her arms around his shoulders, only to jump backwards when the figure's face changed in front of her.

It was the boy's mother, emaciated, broken and crying. Her words were swallowed in sobs.

"I'm sorry."

"Ha-Ha!" cried the child from atop the creature. "I fooled you!"

Gillian stood there – ragged, barefoot and alone – staring up at the creature who towered above her and the child who could just barely be seen on its shoulder.

Please… just don't hurt…

Its tongue shot out, wrapped around her and proceeded to squeeze the breath out of her. Just as she left the ground and was drawn into its mouth, she heard the child scream one last horrifying thing.

"It won't kill you! No one dies here!"

It was a lesson that little Hieronymus Scratch had learned well from his mother: when you become a God, the first thing you banish is mercy.

Epilogue: The Café

Sophie looked at the broken glass on the floor; it wasn't especially interesting, but it kept her from looking at the hole in the wall.

The first time she had done this, she'd been entranced by the entrance into the other world, heard its voice calling her name, and had nearly jumped in after the poor young man she'd pushed in just moments before.

Something... a strange smell that hit her nose just as she leaned inside... had stopped her.

It doesn't want me... but I'm not expendable.

So instead she focused on the broken glass. She got a dust pan and broom and cleaned it up. It was routine for her.

The first time, ten years before, had been bad; she'd panicked once she'd leapt away from the hole. It had occurred to her what she'd done and the gaping maw hungrily swallowing the young man could never be dispelled from her memory. She'd run around the café, knocking over the tables, whimpering with her hands pressed against her mouth in horror at what she had done. She didn't know what was on the other side of the hole and didn't want to know. All she knew was that an entranceway into another world, usually hidden by the portrait, was now clearly visible from the street; anyone walking by would see it! They would call the police and take her away... if she was lucky.

In the darkest part of her imagination, she clearly saw them taking her hand and foot, screaming, to the hole and tossing her in.

No one had walked by.

It had been just like that cop the first time the café called to her, when she had run all the way there in slippers; the cop had seen but hadn't seen. Something told him to look elsewhere and there was no fighting it.

Whenever the horrible thing happened, the café demanded privacy. And it got it.

In ten years, Sophie had learned many things: how to clean up the mess, how not to worry about being caught, how not to ask any questions and, especially, how not to open the book.

When it came down to it, the rules of the world were simple: there were good things and bad things.

Opening the book was a bad thing.

And she would never forget that toughest lesson: how there was no charming creature with Ashton Kutcher's face that would enfold her in its claws and make her Queen of the Underworld as reward for her love and loyalty. No, this café, where the portal to that world was located, is where she would remain until the end of her days.

The palace guard... the keeper of the drawbridge... and she was thankful.

Anything's better than going down that hole.

Sophie went through the same procedure she went through every night to close up the café: the coffee pots and mugs were scrubbed, the register tallied, the mousetraps reloaded. There would be no need to find a new portrait to cover up the hole; there would be a fully restored pen-and-ink rendition of a willow tree bending in a high wind hanging on the wall when she returned the next morning.

She walked around the café one last time, running the "idiot check," making sure that no one had dropped anything of value that would end up in the lost and found drawer. She looked at the bookshelf and spotted the two words printed on the spine:

M
e
m
o
r
i
a
l

T
a
l
e
s

Clean of dust. It would take another year for the dust to build up again and that would be one of things that would attract the next one: the lure of little-told tales, of dark secrets waiting to be discovered.

Some stories should pass away, she thought as she turned away from the shelf. Less than a minute later, she was putting on her coat, shutting off the lights and locking the door behind her.

And year after year, the café opened its door to the grieving and down-at-heart. The coffee and tea were always hot and sweet, the small cakes were soft and fresh, and no one noticed how, once a year, something horrible happened there.

Afterward

In 2003, I finished writing my first novel. It was called *They All Came To The Memorial Café*. It was more than a year in the making. I was so proud to have finished my very first novel.

You'll never read it. It was shit.

Well, *most* of it was shit. I just couldn't see myself publishing the novel as it stood and I didn't want to rewrite it. The novel was about a fiendish typewriter that typed only horrible stories and then made them come true. And while I'm perfectly happy to let the bulk of that book sit unread for the rest of time, there were some pieces of it that begged to be released; some of the stories that came from that infernal typewriter as well as a few of the chapters that stood alone as examples of good writing and an active imagination were worth an airing. I decided to rework those pieces and write some new material in order to build a new short story collection. The idea to reinsert the café and bring all the tales together at the end (by means of a story within a story, so to speak) came later, and I'm so glad that it did.

For those who like a good yarn, the book has already ended. For those who like to look behind the scenes, I've included a few details about how the stories came about:

IT

This is the oldest story in the collection, written when I was still a fresh student at Stonehill College sometime between 1987 and 1991 (the exact year escapes me). Most of the stories I wrote in my youth betray a lack of sophistication that is quite normal in young writers. A look through old notebooks to find tales that would prop up this book yielded very few catches, but this tale still holds up. This tale of a bullied child who gets his revenge (off-screen, so to speak) still speaks to me as the still-bitter victim of educational bullying. The story was published in Stonehill's literary magazine and then later popped up in the aborted *Memorial Café* novel. I'm glad it's finally found a home here.

Brainfood

The will to be a success is great indeed, and sometimes we just don't care who we step on to get what we want, but every action has its consequences. This is the story of a good man who chooses to forget that he's a good man to get ahead. His lapse is brief, but the damage he causes lasts a lifetime.

This was the first new story written for this collection, with a mindset to simply provide a horrible punch line to a simple tale. I think it succeeds.

The Damned Queen

This is another story from the aborted *Memorial Café* novel. The idea to write a story in the style of a fairy tale was appealing and the story was written in three hours on one Sunday afternoon in 2002. It was a pleasure to write and I'm still enamored of it.

Broken Record

Definitely a product of my recent love of Doctor Who. Time travel tales are fascinating because, so many writers have so many rules for time travel, even though there is no such thing. There are some schools that believe that one can not travel through time without adversely affecting the future (such as Ray Bradbury in "A Sound Of Thunder") while others believe that if the universe came to a grinding halt for every little paradox, nothing would ever get done (a paraphrased quote from Douglas Adams). This story came from the attraction of writing a tale from the point of view of someone who hunts and then becomes the hunted, leaving his story unfinished but with the resolution assured nevertheless. It has also occurred to me that this is a Frankenstein story where the creature turns out to be the scientist himself.

Caught Amongst The Banister

A simple ghost story. I suspect that I don't write enough stories from a woman's perspective. But the two things that hold the story together for me are the details that bring a sense of reality to what is an unreal situation (keys, footsteps, shoes, gin) and the relationship between the two women, which has a much closer bond than what would have existed between two men. It's my belief that the relationships that women have with each other are the strongest because adult women share

a willful understanding of each other that doesn't exist even between a
parent and child. The fact that Marybeth keeps Helen's keys, a harsh
reminder of what happened to her friend, tells me more than anything
else about what went through her mind when she found Helen on the
stairway.

Look At Me !

When I moved into my first apartment away from home, my
roommate was, in no uncertain terms, a swine. What stuck out most was
his ability to treat whatever girl he was currently dating badly and his
confidence that she would be back for more. The girls he dated never let
him down. And Yes, he even referred to his penis as his "sauseege." My
personal disgust at his behavior led to this story.

Oddly enough, the night I first thought of this story, I finished
taking a shower and found a long, bleeding scratch on the back of my leg
that I hadn't noticed before. Is it too much to imagine…?

Whatever Happened To Bobby?

A rewritten chapter from the *Memorial Café* novel, I was hesitant
to throw this piece away because I liked that trip down the basement
where Bobby was kept. I also liked the idea of one story commenting on
another. I also love the idea that the things we create in our darkest
memories could somehow take on a life of their own. This, of course,
became the basis for the entire book.

Mommy And The Midnight Caller

Another refugee from the *Memorial Café* novel, this story was the centerpiece, telling the tale of how the novel's chief villain, a young boy, found his destiny. To all budding psychiatrists out there, I'd like to make clear that, as many times as I've been annoyed at my parents, I've never wished a gigantic lizard on them. This story seems to be more about what happens when "might makes right" in parenting mixes with religious fanaticism. This was written long before the country got to know the name of Andrea Yates.

Ultimately, like Bobby from "IT," little Ronnie gets his revenge, but is too young to realize that power corrupts. A villain is a villain, no matter what his motives are, and the type of deadly power he wields finally gave me the spark that allowed me to tie the whole book together in the final story.

The final sentence is a blatant steal from Arthur C. Clark's *2001: A Space Odyssey*. I just couldn't resist it.

Teach Yourself Satanism

Another rewritten chapter from the *Memorial Café* novel. I loved the story of this poor fat young lady who dabbles so ridiculously in the occult until something horrible finally seeks her out. A character piece about a fool who finds what she's looking for, only to realize later (in the book's epilogue) that the world of darkness has no morning.

Only God's To Give

This started as a short script I wrote years ago called "Hyde," about a hitman who injects himself with a serum that turns him into a monster, whereupon he tears his targets to shreds. Recently, I read a review of the old silent film "The Golem" in which the phrase "only God's to give" was used in relation to the human soul (something that the golem lacked). I liked the sound of the phrase and realized that "Hyde" could be adapted to convey this new idea.

I sometimes wonder about the evil that men do and, if they have a soul, how they possibly live with themselves. This story is a possible answer to that question.

Let's Get Dead

Conceived while reading a book of Neil Gaiman's short stories. One story mentioned voodoo powder that rendered a subject seemingly dead. I thought that this might be an idea for a type of drug that might be coveted in a future society.

This story was the most fun to write as it allowed me to let my imagination run wild and to simply make up words, defining them as the story went along. I also like the interruption of the narrative as it felt like a new and different way to tell a story. Some may disagree, but it was fun nevertheless.

More: A Tale Of Capitulation

An example of automatic writing, jotting down the first thing that enters your head. After writing the first few sentences, I returned to the story the next day and decided on a direction for it.

I'm not sure who is more pathetic, the fat woman who is enabled by her adult son or the son who is powerless against his mother's will. They're both prisoners and powerless against one another. Look through any window on your street and see people like these torturing each other. But don't let them see you.

The Button Pusher

This is, quite literally, a story that has been two decades in the making. The bare essentials of the idea were written into my notebook in 1991 and lay dormant until I embarked on *They All Came To The Memorial Café*. Needing a new idea for one of the demonic typewriter's tales, I found those few lines in 2002 and set to work on it. The original story, as written for the novel, had no ending because I did not want the novel to end with worldwide holocaust. The abandonment of that novel allowed me to tie up the story with a final page. I was reading *Don Quixote* at the time and, while leafing through it to find a passage that Dave could read to Tracy, I happened upon Quixote's quote about the giants, about how God would smile on their removal from the Earth, and realized what a wonderfully serendipitous thing that was, considering what Dave had just done to save his girl. I also love the idea of true love blossoming in the most sterile and unlikely of places. "There is beauty in the bellow of the blast" as Sir W.S. Gilbert said and, although he meant it as a joke, I think there is some truth to it.

Into The Deep... The Color Is Black...

The first five pages of this story were originally how this book opened, but I felt it was taking too long to get to "the good stuff." This was a problem, as I believed the reader needed to know a thing or two about Gillian in order for the ending to work. I realized that by reprising the book's opening paragraph in this story, I could move all the background info about Gillian to this story and capture the reader early on with a quick prologue.

The toughest thing about this book was trying to write a final story that would convey that the reader themselves had, in a way, entered the action the way Gillian did, that the act of actually reading *Memorial Tales* had made her one of the characters and subject to the will of an unbalanced mind (Hieronymus Scratch or Craig O'Connor... you be the judge). It was my hope that this would turn what was once a novel made of disparate stories into something more interesting. It would be marvelous if I could somehow produce a copy of this book especially tuned to each reader, with their own names in the place of Gillian's and putting them in her place as she is swallowed up by the café and confronts little Ronnie's creature, but that is not the way we do things in literature. So poor Gillian Gardner is served up as a sacrifice in lieu of the reader, who can read from the safety of their own home with the knowledge that she is suffering in their place.

Gillian's ordeal is a heavy rewrite of the climax of *They All Came To The Memorial Café*.

Taking into account the work on the never-published novel and that some of these stories date back to the 20th century, this book has been twenty years in the making. It was good to finally lay this ghost to rest, to give these tales a home, and to hopefully give you something to think about (and maybe shudder about). If I have introduced at least one nightmare into at least one reader's sleep, then it has all been worth it.

Until next time, Goodnight.

Craig O'Connor
Brockton, MA
October 9, 2011

Craig O'Connor is a writer from New England who specializes in suspense tales and murder mysteries. *Memorial Tales* is his second collection of short stories. He is the creator of "Icky" Mickey Turner, the protagonist of his two mystery novels, *The Whitechapel Five* and *The Monster Of Modern Times*.

Portions of this book were written in Massachusetts at the Ames Free Library in Easton and Owen O'Leary's Pub in Brockton. Read the book again and guess where each portion was written.